Lionel of the Sea.

Sea.

———BY A POPULAR AUTHOR.——— —

London:

CHARLES FOX, 4, SHOE LANE, FLEET STREET, E.C.

LIONEL OF THE SEA.

A STORY OF THE DAYS OF CAPTAIN KYDD.

CHAPTER I.

THE DEFIANCE—THE STORM AND THE SPECTRE ON THE REEF.

"FLING me overboard if you will, cast me to the mercy of the foaming billows if you like, and my last cry as I plunge beneath them shall be my bitterest curse! And now, ere I am gone, you shall hear how I hate—loathe—detest—abhor and scorn you, and you shall see that the poor and nameless ocean foundling has at least sufficient spirit to hurl his defiance in the very teeth of the dreaded pirate. Yes! here on his own deck, and surrounded by his bloodthirsty crew."

This vehement outburst proceeded from the lips of a youth, who stood upon the quarterdeck of a very beautifully built schooner.

His eyes flashed with anger—his cheeks flushed, and from head to foot he quivered with the intensity of his emotions, as he shook his fist at the celebrated pirate before whom he had been summoned.

With his right hand—the fingers of which sparkled and blazed with jewels—resting lightly on the butt of one of the ornamental pistols stuck in his belt, Captain Kydd regarded the speaker with a black and threatening scowl.

A number of fierce-looking pirates were gathered round the two, and as the boy's words rang over the deck their eyes gleamed forth their latent fires, while ready hands sought dirk and pistol.

Lionel-of-the-Sea—for such was the appropriate epithet which more than twelve years previously Captain Kydd had bestowed upon him—flinched not.

He reared his noble head aloft, and shook his long and curling yellow hair, as a lion shakes his mane, while he still extended his arm and fist before him.

"Boy," thundered Captain Kydd, "what madness is this! Go instantly and do my bidding. I again command you."

"And I again refuse," retorted Lionel-of-the-Sea. "Why do you wish me to imbrue these hands in the life stream of one who has never done me the slightest injury? Why, when this accursed craft swarms with men who pant for blood like tigers, do you select me to be the one to creep down yonder hatch on tip-toe and enter the cabin of the stranger, who appeared in so unaccountable a manner amongst us, and strike a dirk into his heart as he sleeps? Tell me?"

Captain Kydd replied not.

The crew preserved a breathless silence.

A sharp, wild, and scornful laugh broke from Lionel's lips.

"You answer not," cried the youth. "Listen, and I will tell you. You wish to force me to do it, Captain Kydd, because you know that aboard the Vampire there is not one man, even including the ferocious Nero and yourself, who for his life's sake dare enter the after-cabin while that mysterious man is there. No! Lionel-of-the-Sea alone would make the venture; but he tells you to your teeth that neither persuasion, threat, nor bribe will ever induce him to stain his soul with murder."

Captain Kydd trembled with suppressed fury.

Then there stepped from behind the pirate captain a tall and muscular negro.

He was very gorgeously attired.

Upon his head he wore a red fez cap embroidered and tasselled with gold.

A short sleeveless jacket of the same rich colour, and ornamented, not only with gold lace, but also with jewels, descended to his waist, round which was swathed a striped sash.

The latter supported a brace of pistols, a kreese, and a very handsome scimitar, sheathed in a case of crimson velvet, mounted with gold.

The hilt of this weapon positively blazed with jewels.

A white tunic, reaching to his knees, and a pair of sea boots completed his attire.

A low, fierce, gutteral exclamation broke from his lips as he glared at our hero and unsheathed his kreese.

Quick as thought our hero drew from his belt one of the long-barrelled pistols he invariably carried there, and held it in a direct line with the negro's eye.

A muttered imprecation escaped the baffled black.

"Ferocious," growled the negro lieutenant. "Who says he is ferocious?"

"He is not only ferocious, but he is a coward into the bargain," retorted Lionel-of-the-Sea, as the ominous click of his pistol jarred upon the negro's ear.

"You think I am afraid," growled the negro. "But Nero fears nothing."

"He fears me," said our hero, with something like a sneer, "and he is afraid of the stranger who has so unceremoniously taken up his abode in the after-cabin."

"It is a lie," hissed the lieutenant. "See."

And clutching the hilt of his kresse convulsively he withdrew from the range of our hero's pistol, and proceeded with stealthy steps towards the hatchway.

A low cheer came from the assembled pirates.

Lionel coolly replaced his pistol in his belt.

"Are you satisfied now, Captain Kydd? You might have saved all this bother by offering Nero the alternative of going below or hanging up above."

And he pointed to the yard-arm.

Captain Kydd spoke not.

And now the attention of all was withdrawn from our hero and directed towards the hatchway down which Nero had vanished.

There was a silence of something like two minutes, during which no one seemed either to move or to breathe.

Then a terrific yell echoed through the ship.

The next moment the gigantic form of Nero emerged with precipitate haste from the hatchway.

Indeed, so great was his hurry that he stumbled and almost fell as he reached the upper deck.

One or two of the pirates rushed to his assistance.

"Well," demanded Lionel-of-the-Sea, with a tinge of irony in his voice, "have you succeeded, Nero? Is the incomprehensible stranger disposed of?"

The eyes of the black lieutenant rolled horribly in his head as he glared round, like one both baffled and bewildered.

"Is he dead?" asked Captain Kydd.

"No," yelled Nero, in reply, and he shook so in every joint that it was only with the greatest difficulty he could preserve his footing. "He is gone!"

"Gone!" echoed Captain Kydd. "Impossible. Gone! I'll not believe it. Institute a thorough search immediately."

This was an order the pirates did not exactly relish.

Nevertheless they dispersed, and running hither and thither, helter-skelter, commenced to ransack every portion of the ship.

Meanwhile our hero and Captain Kydd maintained their positions on the quarter-deck, exchanging glances of defiance and hatred.

"Boy," hissed Captain Kydd, "that you know more of this matter than I shall ever be able to wring from you I feel perfectly convinced. How did this mysterious individual come to be on board my vessel?"

"I know not," replied our hero, stoutly.

"And where has he gone to now?" yelled the pirate.

"To that question," replied our hero, "I return the same answer—I know not."

"Death and fury!" panted Captain Kydd, and his white teeth gleamed viciously beneath his black moustachios, while his fingers convulsively clutched the butt of one of his pistols, "you shall suffer for this. Ah!"

This latter exclamation was called forth by Nero, who, rushing up excitedly, glared first at the captain and then at our hero.

"Well," demanded Captain Kydd, "what is the result of your search?"

"He is gone, undoubtedly," replied the black, darting a malicious look at Lionel.

"But where?" demanded Captain Kydd.

"Ask that tiger's cub," replied Nero, indicating our hero with his kreese: "he knows."

"It is false," replied Lionel-of-the-Sea.

There was a rush of feet.

Then up the ladder and on to the quarter deck came tumbling a number of pirates, waving their arms frantically, and otherwise indulging in such gestures as betokened that they were labouring under intense excitement.

"Overboard with him—cut his throat—brain him—hoist him up to the yard-arm—riddle him with shot."

These and a hundred other suggestions of a similar kind were yelled forth by the now frantic ruffians, who seemed to be worked up to a pitch of frenzy that had actually maddened them.

Lionel-of-the-Sea stepped back a pace or two, and with a calm and dignified air drew from his belt the two pistols it supported.

One he pointed at Captain Kydd.

The other at the crew of howling miscreants, who were thus urgently demanding his murder.

"Stand back!" cried Lionel-of-the-Sea, with clear ringing voice and fearless front, "or I discharge both these pistols at once, and Lionel-of-the-Sea never misses his mark!"

As he made this assertion our hero darted a significant glance at Captain Kydd.

"Hark!" cried the latter, holding up his hands.

The low, muffled rumbling of thunder afar off boomed over the darkly-rolling billows, the whitely-foaming tops of which glistened with that phosphorescent light which always indicates the rapid approach of a furious tempest.

All started.

So wholly occupied had been the pirate crew during the past hour that not one of them had noticed that the sky had been rapidly growing dark, and that the billows, which had been rolling heavily all day, increased in magnitude each minute.

Simultaneously they awakened to the fact that the Vampire was in peril.

"All hands aloft," cried Captain Kydd; "take in every scrap of canvas. By heaven! we shall be overset in another minute."

As he spoke the Vampire lurched to leeward until her lower sails were dipped in the foaming brine.

A red and forked flash of lightning descended into the seething waters.

"All hands aloft," shrieked the black lieutenant. "But first, boys, fling this son of Satan into the waves. We shall never weather the storm if Lionel-of-the-Sea is permitted to remain on board."

"Rocks ahead," sang out the man at the masthead.

Another blaze of lightning lit up the scene, and Captain Kydd, as he shaded his eyes with his hand, saw, but a short distance before them, a sharp and jagged coral reef, round the base of which the waves raved and beat with redoubled fury.

The direction of the ship was instantly altered, and as she reeled through the blackened waters a loud crash was heard overhead.

With a noise not unlike that of thunder the foretopsail split into shreds before the fury of a sudden gust of wind which swept over the ocean.

"Quick!" cried Captain Kydd. "All hands aloft!"

"Overboard with him," screamed the furious negro.

And he rushed upon our hero.

He was followed by a score or more of the pirates, while their comrades commenced to mount the rigging with all possible speed.

There was another flash of lightning.

A rattling peal of thunder instantaneously succeeded it.

Then followed two bright red flashes and two clear and sharp reports.

Our hero had been as good as his word.

He had discharged his pistols.

Captain Kydd staggered back several paces.

The foremost pirate uttered a yell, leapt into the air, and then fell sprawling on the deck.

This feat was greeted with such a howl as might have issued from the throats of a pack of wolves as the pirates rushed upon Lionel in a body.

He was instantly dashed to the deck.

Then Nero raised him bodily in his brawny arms, as if he had been a baby, and with one effort hurled him over the bulwarks.

The splash which followed was drowned by the clamour of the tempest.

"Ha! ha!" laughed the black, in horrible glee, "he is gone. Now, boys, to work, or we shall be gone too."

The pirates gave a cheer.

It had a very strange and unnatural sound, however.

Then they dispersed.

"You are wounded, captain," said Nero, advancing towards Kydd.

"'Tis nothing," replied the pirate captain. "It shall be seen to anon. You had better go aft."

Nero sheathed his knife and hastened away.

The Vampire lurched again.

Captain Kydd reeled, nearly lost his footing, and then just saved himself by clutching a rope.

His wound was more serious than he cared to acknowledge.

Then—as wit groaning timbers, rattling yards, and creaking masts, the Vampire staggered through the raging waters, right past the coral reef, to which they were even now so close that it seemed as if they avoided it by little else than absolute chance—a perfect blaze of lightning, descending from a black and tempest-gathered cloud, lit up the scene for a space of time, during which fifteen might have been counted rapidly.

That lingering and brilliant blaze of electric light revealed to Captain Kydd a sight which seemed to root him to the deck with mingled terror and amazement.

A cry of horror echoed from fore to aft, and the pirates up aloft amid the rigging joined in the discordant chorus of their comrades on deck.

And every startled face was turned in one direction.

That was towards the coral reef.

There, standing upon the sharp and rugged peak, with his cloak streaming and fluttering from his shoulders like a banner, was a weird and spectral figure.

His costume was that exceedingly elegant one adopted by English cavaliers during the reign of the unfortunate Charles the First.

In his right hand he flourished a naked sword.

In his left, which was raised in the air, he held something he shook with mocking defiance at Captain Kydd.

That something was a large sealed packet.

"Vanderdecken!" shrieked Captain Kydd.

A shout of horror and dismay made itself heard above the clash and roar of the tempest.

Another flash of lightning, more brilliant and of yet longer duration than the previous one, again flickered upon the ocean.

It played with a strange effect over and around the coral reef.

On the top still stood the spectral figure, with his cloak fluttering, his sword gleaming, and the sealed packed held tauntingly aloft.

At the base clung the form of one well-known to Captain Kydd and his murderous crew.

It was Lionel-of-the-Sea!

There was a momentary lull in the fury of the tempest.

A taunting laugh rang over the waves.

Captain Kydd uttered a fearful imprecation, and levelled his pistol at the apparition on the reef.

There was a flash and a bang.

Captain Kydd had fired!

CHAPTER II.

CAPTAIN KYDD ATTACKS A DUTCH TRADER, AND HANS VAN RYDER PROVES HIMSELF A HERO.

THE lightning blazed down upon the scene once more.

The pirates strained their starting eyeballs towards the coral reef.

But the spectre had vanished.

Lionel-of-the-Sea had also disappeared.

The seething waters roared and raved around the base of the reef, and almost without intermission the electric flashes glittered over the peak.

But no trace of the phantom Vanderdecken or of Lionel-of-the-Sea could be discovered.

"They are gone," gasped Captain Kydd, with unutterable relief.

"Your pistol blew the spectre away," said Nero, with a grin. "And as for young Lionel, the waves have swallowed him."

Captain Kydd now turned his attention to the safety of his vessel, and right gallantly did the saucy schooner do battle with the raging elements.

But gradually the warfare of nature ceased.

The storm became hushed.

The raging winds unclasped the billows.

The lightning no longer leapt along the heavens and the thunder peals ceased to crash and reverberate overboard.

In the course of two hours, so altered and so complete was the change which came over the aspect of the ocean, that no one would have imagined that so short a time before it had been the scene of such terrific strife.

A peaceful calm settled on the ocean.

The turbulent clouds cleared away, and left a bright blue sky.

Over the vast expanse of water a ship was sighted dancing gaily on the rippling waves.

A trim and neat-looking craft, lightly rigged, and with every stitch of canvas set to court the gentle breeze.

Captain Kydd's attention was called to the strange sail by a man aloft on the look out.

The pirate chief took up his telescope, and placing it at his eye, looked long and earnestly at the approaching vessel.

"What do you make her out, captain ?" asked Nero, who stood by his side.

"A merchantman, I should say by her rig," replied Kydd ; "but for the soul of me I can't make out where she hails from."

Nero took the glass and placed it to his eye.

"She is a larger craft than our own," he observed, scanning the distant ship intently. "The Zuyder Zee," he added, suddenly ; "I see her name distinctly on her bows. A Dutch trader, for a wager, and perhaps carrying a valuable cargo."

"True, true ; we will overhaul her, at any rate," said Captain Kydd, with fiendish joy. "At the helm there ! Luff two points, so that every sail will draw. That course will head her off more completely, too, Nero. See that the guns are got ready, and prepare for a stiff engagement. These Dutchmen are stubborn devils when driven in a corner, and know how to fight."

"Aye, aye, sir ; we'll be prepared for them."

The negro gave orders for the guns to be charged with grape-shot, and have the ship prepared for a warm engagement.

Now call the men to quarters, that their arms may be well seen to, and then run up our flag. This fellow may as well know who he has to meet, and make up his mind to take in sail and come to terms, for no ship afloat can escape the speed of the Vampire.

Nero gave the order, which brought the men to quarters, and then hoisted the piratical flag to the masthead.

"Is the midship gun loaded ?" asked Captain Kydd.

"It is, sir."

"Then let the gunner fire a salute when you show our colours."

"Ho ! gunner, a match for the midship gun, and look sharp ; there is a lot of work to be done," cried Nero, joyously, for, like his commander, he was always happy at the prospect of a sanguinary encounter.

The gunner was speedily at his post with fuse and match, and soon the thunder of the heavy artillery rolled like distant thunder over the rippling sea.

At the same time the flag was unfurled and fluttered in the breeze, showing the hideous device of a skull and cross-bones in white on a black ground.

Captain Kydd, with his eye to the glass, watched the other vessel to see what effect the roar of the gun and sight of the flag would have.

"The varlets have changed their course, and mean to give us a run," he said, with a grim laugh. "They might as well try to reach the clouds as to escape the claws of the Vampire. Ha ! ha !"

This fact the Dutchman soon became aware of.

The Vampire spanked through the billows in gallant style, and every minute encroached perceptibly upon the stranger.

Still the Zuyder Zee showed no signs of surrender. She kept on her course with every stitch of canvas she was capable of carrying stretched to the breeze.

She rode gracefully as a swan over the rolling billows, but her progress was slow compared to that of the Vampire.

Captain Kydd watched his prey with the eye of a hawk, calculating the minutes when he would be able to pounce upon her.

Presently he saw between twenty and thirty men, civilians and sailors, bustling about the deck.

"The varlets are preparing to give us battle," he cried, taking another look at the stranger through his glass. "Send a round shot athwart her bows to let them know we are ready for them."

This order was promptly obeyed by willing hands, and a minute later a single shot was sent plunging into the sea just ahead of the Zuyder Zee.

"Just as I thought," said the pirate captain. "They are clearing the deck for action. We've got stubborn rascals to fight, men, and unless we make short work of it when we get our grappling irons on her, not many of you will live to share the booty she carries. By heaven, what vision of loveliness is that !"

This exclamation was caused as he caught sight of a fair young creature, who stood on the deck of the stranger amidst the bustle of excited men, clinging tearfully to the arm of a handsome youth, who was evidently trying to induce her to go below.

"I never saw a creature so beautiful," Nero observed, taking a look at her through the captain's glass. "So young, so fair, so supple. A prize worth winning. Something to charm the soul and wile away the dreary hours in fervent bliss."

"She shall be mine !" exclaimed Captain Kydd.

The pirate barque had by this time got within speaking distance of the Dutch trader.

Her crew of swarthy cut-throats literally crowded her deck, bristling with murderous weapons, all eager for the ensanguined fray which was about to take place.

The gunners stood ready with lighted fuse to send forth the destructive missiles at the word of command.

No shot as yet was fired on either side.

One was evidently waiting to see what the other would do.

As the vessels neared each other to about a cable's length the Vampire was brought on the same course with the Dutch trader.

"Ship ahoy !" shouted Captain Kydd from the bows.

"What do you want ?" cried the captain of the trader, in broken English.

"Lay to ; we want to come aboard."

"Go to the devil, cut-throat."

"Surrender, or I will blow you out of the water !" yelled Captain Kydd, with a fierce oath.

"Surrender is a word I have not learnt the

meaning of," returned the Dutch captain, with a defiant look. "and your threats will not frighten me."

"Open with your guns, men," cried the pirate captain, furiously, "and punish the varlet for his arrogance."

Instantly the order was obeyed. A long gun and four small carronades belched forth their contents of death.

Terrible was the havoc carried among the crew so close at hand.

While yet the sound of the firing resounded in the air, a similar shower of deadly missiles came hurling from the deck of the Dutchman, dealing fearful destruction amongst the mass of blood-thirsty wretches on the Vampire.

The yells of maddened, and shrieks of wounded men, made a fearful cadence to the thunder of the guns.

Quivering from stem to stern, both vessels sped on for awhile almost side by side, their guns belching forth sheets of fire and showers of deadly missiles.

How fearfully the work of dire destruction was carried on was seen in the torn sails, splintered spars, and huge gaps in the shattered bulwarks.

Then Captain Kydd, his face tigerish in remorseless ferocity, heading his desperate crew, leaped upon the mid-deck of the ill-fated Dutch trader.

Close at his heels and crowding on either side of him came his friends—human they were not in look or deed, but they came in merciless fury, as come the rolling billows dashing against the mighty rock, which rears its breast to stay their course—upon a phlanax of bright steel weapons, held in sturdy hands, by men as brave as they, and not unnerved by conscious crime or weakened by excess or dissipation.

Captain Kydd, with compressed lips and a light of deadly vengeance in his eyes, went in quest of the Dutch captain, who had hurled defiance in his teeth.

The commander of the trader stood in the thick of the fight, wielding a ponderous old cavalry sword, which he used with deadly effect upon all who came within his reach.

By his side stood the brave youth, undaunted by the overwhelming number of the foe, who continued to swarm over the vessel's side in spite of the courageous resistance offered by the Dutch sailors and the male passengers.

"I fear we are fighting a hopeless battle," said the Dutch captain, "we are outnumbered by at least four to one, and already half of our ship-mates have fallen."

"True!" replied the boy, with quiet determination, "if it is ordained that we too must fall, let us avenge the death of our friends, and have the satisfaction of sending as many as possible of these merciless devils to perdition, while we have the strength to raise an arm. Ah! that for you."

The youth parried a rapid lunge delivered by a ferocious-looking pirate, then he leaped suddenly forward, and by a dexterous turn of his wrist he wrenched the weapon from the ruffian's grasp;

the next moment the pirate fell with a cloven skull.

Already there were at least a dozen bodies in a heap at the feet of the Dutch captain and his young companion—the work of one man and a boy!

Suddenly above the fearful din of battle was heard a roar like that of a tiger, and the next moment Captain Kydd dashed at the Dutch commander.

"Die, insolent varlet," he yelled.

Up went his gleaming blade to strike a death blow.

"Not yet, fiend," retorted the Dutch captain, scornfully, "and when my time comes, I shall not fall by your hand."

Captain Kydd's impetuous blow was parried and turned aside by the Dutchman, and he jumped back just in time to avoid being impaled on the blade of the long cavalry sword.

He had found a foeman worthy of his steel, one he saw he would have to be careful of.

The captain of the trader was a tall, thick-set man, of powerful build, with broad shoulders and brawny arms, and his ponderous weapon darted about, flashing like forked lightning.

With a grim smile on his face he took two steps after Captain Kydd.

"You would kill me," he said. "Let me try your prowess hand to hand."

The pirate captain went back, his face distorted with baffled fury.

"Men to the rescue of your leader," he called.

More than a dozen of the blood-stained wretches came bounding forward in answer to the summons, howling like a pack of savage beasts.

"At him, men! Cut them down; give no quarter," exclaimed Captain Kydd, foaming with malignant wrath.

The savage pirates, uttering yells of vengeance, dashed at the brave commander of the trader, pressing in all round him.

The youth saw the danger of his father, and was about to leap in among the merciless crew when a piercing scream broke from a woman's lips.

"Hans van Ryder! Hans, where are you?" came in supplicating accents.

The youth turned and saw the beautiful girl, who had infatuated Captain Kydd, rushing wildly towards him with a terror-stricken look on her fair young face.

"Miss Everleigh, Violet! why have you exposed yourself to the horrors and dangers of this fearful scene?" he said, as she came staggering up to his side.

"I could not remain below while this fearful carnage was going on," she faltered, closing her eyes to shut out the awful sight that surrounded her. "Oh! how will all this end!"

"By the slaughter of every man on one side or the other," replied the youth, encircling her trembling form with his left arm.

Even as he spoke a sharp cry of agony rang above the clash of steel, and sent a chill to the heart of Hans van Ryder.

"Heavens!" he exclaimed, "the monsters have stricken my father unto death. Revenge!"

Supporting the beautiful form of Miss Everleigh, he hurried to where the last scene of this horrible tragedy was being enacted.

His blood-reeking weapon descended as he broke into the remnant of the villanous crew, who had surrounded his father, and a pirate fell at his feet with his skull cloven in twain.

He saw his father on the blood-weltering deck writhing in the last throes of death.

The sight drove him mad with desperation, and he flew at the ensanguined ruffians with the ferocity of a tiger.

Two more men fell beneath his lightning blade, and the remaining pirates dashed upon him uttering cries of vengeance.

Encumbered as he was with the inanimate form of Miss Everleigh, he stood a poor chance against the infuriated ruffians who attacked him without fear of death, but he held his own bravely, though his arm began to ache and his brain was in a whirl of excitement.

A quick sharp blow from the negro's heavy sword disarmed the gallant boy.

Then the blood-stained weapons of his foemen were raised to hack him to pieces.

"Hold your hands!" cried Captain Kydd, in time to save the boy's life. "The young spitfire has the courage of a lion, and I would make him one of us."

"That you never will," cried the youth, boldly, "so you may as well drive a sword through my heart at once, and let me join my murdered father. Death would be far more preferable to me than life with you."

"Bah! you will think different when you are calmer."

"Never!"

"We shall see. Nero, take that girl and put her in my private cabin. Two of you secure the boy and put him in the hold of the Vampire. If in time he does not accept my terms he shall hang from the yard-arm."

This order was readily obeyed. Two of the ruffians seized the boy from behind and pinioned his arms.

Nero took the beautiful Violet Everleigh in his brawny arms and carried her away.

The heroic boy was dragged after her by his captors to a doom worse than death, yet his brave heart did not quail at the torture he felt was in store for him, as he was determined not to become a pirate.

CHAPTER III.

LIONEL-OF-THE-SEA FINDS HIMSELF IN A WORLD OF MYSTERIES.

FOR a short time we must leave the vessel captured by Captain Kydd, and return to our hero, Lionel-of-the-Sea.

When Lionel was hurled over the bulwarks by the savage black lieutenant, Nero, the lad found himself going down in the black seething waters.

He thought that his last moment had come, but he had no fear of death, preferring it to disgrace.

A thundering noise rang in his ears, his mouth filled with salt water, and his brain seemed ready to burst.

In his agony he flung his arms above his head, and that action caused him to ascend swiftly towards the surface.

Lionel was a good swimmer, but what chance had he, a lad, against the ocean lashed to fury by the storm.

The heart of the strongest and bravest man would have quailed at such a position, and when Lionel, drawing in a deep breath, opened his eyes and saw nothing but heaving mountains round him, he crossed his hands humbly on his breast and waited for the end.

By the mighty roaring and crashing he knew that there were rocks not far away, and the next wave might hurl him like a fragment of weed upon some jagged point, and tear him to atoms.

Lionel-of-the-Sea gave up all hope, for indeed his case seemed hopeless, and shutting out the awful sight from his eyes he lay perfectly still, when a strong yet gentle hand was laid upon his shoulder, and he felt that he was raised above the waves.

For a moment Lionel thought that this sensation, for it was indeed a strange one, must be the supreme moment of life passing away into the grim embrace of death, but a loud voice assured him that such was not the case, and that he was saved.

"Courage, lad!" said the voice. "Neither storm nor wave can hurt you now. I am Vanderdecken."

Lionel-of-the-Sea opened his eyes, and discovered that he was resting on a ledge of rock, against which the foam-capped billows hurled themselves in impotent fury.

He was saved from a violent and awful death, but the appearance of his preserver filled him with horror, and sent a thrill through every nerve.

Tall and commanding was the figure of Vanderdecken, and *white* from head to foot.

He wore a broad sombrero hat upon his head, from which flowed long streams of unkempt hair.

His heavily-moustached face was grave, yet kind in expression, and lit up by his eyes, which gleamed and glinted as he glanced from the bay to the Vampire, rolling heavily in the trough of the sea.

A loose robe hung from his shoulders down to his knees, from which descended a pair of long loose boots.

"Courage, lad," he said again.

Then he extended his gauntleted hand towards the Vampire, and gave vent to a loud mocking laugh.

"Once more I have foiled you, Captain Kydd, pirate and villain," he shouted. "Mark me well, Vanderdecken will follow you to the end of the world and thwart all your evil designs. Go! the time is not ripe for you to come within my reach, but your fate is written in the irrevocable book of destiny."

At this moment there was a terrible blaze of lightning; a crash of thunder seemed to tear the very rocks from their foundation, and Lionel-of-the-Sea swooned.

Some time must have elapsed before he came to his senses, for it was now early morning.

The sun was shining brightly, and by the musical murmur of the waves Lionel knew that the storm had passed entirely away.

CHAPTER IV.

THE VISION.

BUT where was Lionel-of-the-Sea? "Surely," he thought, as he glanced round him, "I must be dreaming."

He rubbed his eyes, raised himself on his elbow, and gazed in astonishment, not unmixed with awe, at the luxurious bed on which he was reclining, and the superb appointments of the room.

The richly tapestried walls were hung with shields and burnished weapons.

On a sideboard stood some golden vessels, and near an open window sat what Lionel-of-the-Sea at first took for a heathen idol, snatched at some time from the temple of a savage foe.

But this figure suddenly moved, and standing erect revealed the face of a good-humoured negro, who, approaching the bed, said gleefully—

"Young massa much berrer now. So glad."

"Where am I? What has happened?" Lionel demanded in a breath. "What is the name of this place; and who is the owner of it?"

"Dem am questions dat dis chile no answer for him life," the negro responded. "Jes you drink some ob dis wine, and hab anoder lilly sleep, den p'raps you know all."

"Well," said Lionel, who could not help feeling amused in spite of all his perplexity, "perhaps you will not mind telling me what your name is, and why you are in attendance upon me?"

"Strikes me," said the negro, who had turned to reach a golden goblet filled with an amber-hued liquid, "dat your mem'ry not good. Hab you fogotten dat lilly swim in de sea. You hab to tank your ole frens, Capen Kydd and him lieutenant Nero, for dat."

"Ah! I remember that," Lionel-of-the-Sea said, pressing his hand to his brow; "and I also recollect what followed. But this," with another glance round the room, "is not satisfactory."

"You will find dat dis is," the negro said, as he approached our hero with the goblet on a salver. "Drink, massa."

"But you have not told me your name yet."

"Drink fust, massa, and den dis nigger answer any question you like."

Lionel-of-the-Sea raised the goblet to his lips, and quaffed the delicious fluid.

Instantly he felt that he was drifting back again into unconsciousness.

He seemed to be in a ferry boat gliding along a river as bright and shining as silver.

Sweet strains of music were borne to his ears, a delicious fragrance filled his nostrils, and then all was oblivion.

Again he opened his eyes.

The sun was setting, and the room was flushed with a ruby light.

The negro was nowhere to be seen, and Lionel-of-the-Sea, who now felt as strong and well as he had ever done in his life, sat up and drew back the curtains from the bed.

He started violently as he saw Vanderdecken standing before him.

"Mysterious being," Lionel-of-the-Sea said, "if you are mortal, tell me something of yourself, and why—"

Vanderdecken lifted his hand and silenced the lad.

"Ask me no questions," the weird figure now interposed. "I am no spectre, yet I am not mortal. My touch is as a man's. See! Here is my hand. Grasp it, and do not be afraid."

Lionel did as he was requested, and found that the grasp he encountered was warm and hearty.

"Yonder," said Vanderdecken, stretching his hand towards the open window, "is the ocean. This place is one of my homes. I keep it for fugitives, for waifs of the sea, such as I found you. What is your age, Lionel?"

"I am in my fifteenth year."

"And you were a mere child when you found yourself with Captain Kydd."

"I do not remember by what means I was delivered to his care," Lionel replied.

Vanderdecken smiled, and, turning his head, seemed to be addressing somebody.

"Rise, Lionel," he said, fixing his keen eyes on the boy. "You will find wearing apparel and all necessaries in yonder chest."

Lionel-of-the-Sea averted his eyes for a moment, and when he turned again to Vanderdecken the mysterious being had vanished.

"What trickery is this?" Lionel said, aloud.

"No trickery," said the voice of Vanderdecken. "When you are ready open the door, and you will find me."

Lionel opened the chest and found suits of clothes of all sizes and of the richest materials.

Choosing some garments he commenced to dress, and leaving him to complete his toilet we will follow Vanderdecken.

The house, if it can be so called, was hewn out of a gigantic rock, just such a place as the Norsemen of old used to dwell in.

It was a natural fortress, which no enemy would dream of assailing, for the sea lapped its very windows, which were provided with strong sliding shutters to keep out the effects of wind and water, and were also loopholed to admit of defence.

A second series of shutters of slenderer make ran in grooves over the loopholes when they were not required, so all was secure against the attack of man and the elements.

In fine weather these windows were flung open, and revealed splendid views of the ocean, and Vanderdecken now stood at one of these apertures, gazing at the sun as it dipped down like a huge ball of fire into the ocean.

"Strange that this boy should come into my hands after so many years," he said. "Heaven be praised for that."

Then his whole aspect altered.

His eyes grew dim, tears hot and blinding fell from them, and his whole frame became racked with a paroxysm of grief terrible to see.

"Will my weary pilgrimage never come to an end?" he cried, clasping his hands. "Will the sins of my youth never be atoned for? All such good actions as I am able to perform, and do perform with true penitence in my heart, hold as nought. No, no, I cannot believe that. But answer, ye powers of love and mercy, when shall I be free?"

The only answer he received was the echo of his own distressed voice and the murmur of the sea.

The sun went down, and the great vault of heaven deepened in colour.

Then Vanderdecken turned sadly away from the window, and, descending a flight of stairs, entered a richly-furnished room.

His footsteps were noiseless, and did not disturb a man, about thirty-five years of age, who sat in an attitude of deep thought.

His open hands rested upon his knees, and his head was bowed to his breast.

"What," said Vanderdecken, "still dreaming of the past?"

The man started, but seeing who was before him, rose to his feet, and smiled as he put out his hand.

"How can I forget it?" he said.

"Is there no future?" Vanderdecken demanded, almost sternly. "Look at me—take me as your warning. When I was your age—ah! me, that is long, long ago—I suffered wrong, and in my agony, my foolishness, and want of belief, I turned away from the path which the light of heaven shines upon. Look at me, and take warning."

"I lack no faith, but what can the future be to me, save dark and dreary," the other replied. "Even the night stands before me like a veiled phantom, giving no notion of what is beneath the folds of its sombre garments. If you can tell me aught, I beg, nay, I pray that you will do so."

Vanderdecken's eyes glowed like living coals.

"Another error," he said; "you pray to me! Look above for help. I am but a poor instrument doomed to tread the earth and sail the ocean until such time as my term of punishment may cease."

"But," urged the young man, "you have a power that is not given to mortals. If you can show me nothing of the future, take me back into the past! Show me how it was that my wife perished, and my child—"

"Lived," Vanderdecken interposed.

"So you have told me," the man said, "but that is poor comfort at the best. Pardon, I am most ungrateful."

If Vanderdecken heard these words, he pretended not to hear them.

"I can grant you your wish," he said. "Turn your face to the wall, and on your life do not look round till I bid you."

The young man did so, and as he remained in that attitude deep silence reigned in the apartment.

"Behold!" Vanderdecken cried, suddenly. "This is but a vision of what has been. Read something in it for your future guidance."

Before the open window floated a vapour of ghastly hue, and across it some figures flitted.

"Captain Kydd!" the young man cried. "He holds my child aloft in triumph. His villanous crew crowd round and grin in fiendish delight. But where, where is my wife?"

"Seek her amid the starlight," said Vanderdecken, and in a solemn tone of voice.

The young man clenched his hands and started forward, but Vanderdecken seized him by the throat and held him firmly back.

"Advance a step," Vanderdecken hissed, "and you destroy yourself and all your hopes."

His grasp relaxed as the young man sank back swooning, and then in a moment the vision passed away and gave place to the pale light of the moon.

Little dreaming of what had been taking place, Lionel-of-the-Sea, now fully dressed, stood with his hand resting on the door.

He hesitated before opening it, for the place, although so silent and mysterious, seemed to be filled with whispers.

"If I don't make a start," he said, ashamed of his own weakness, "I may stay here all night."

So saying he threw the door open, and beheld Vanderdecken leaning against a balustrade of black twisted oak.

"Follow me," Vanderdecken said. "Give me your hand if you fear to fall."

"I have no fear," Lionel replied. "Lead me where you will, I have good reason to trust you with all my heart."

Vanderdecken mounted a few steps, and coming to a standstill on a landing, pressed his hand against the wall.

A secret door slid back, and Lionel-of-the-Sea found himself gazing down at the ocean.

"Ask of me any favour in my power, and it shall be granted," Vanderdecken said.

"Can you transport me back to the Vampire?" Lionel asked.

"I can."

"And will?"

"And will," Vanderdecken rejoined. "Let me blindfold your eyes. That is a condition I must enforce."

Lionel-of-the-Sea submitted to this ceremony, and immediately he felt that he was being borne away.

Presently he heard the splashing of oars, as they rose and fell into the sea, and the rim of a drinking vessel touched his lips.

"When next you see light," Vanderdecken said, "you will be almost face to face with Captain Kydd. Great and good work will be in store for you. Do your duty, and do it well. Fear not, and I will ever be at your side."

As Lionel-of-the-Sea heard the last word he sank into a deep sleep.

CHAPTER V.

LIONEL-OF-THE-SEA AND VIOLET EVERLEIGH.

"Come Violet," the pirate has just said, "there is no need for fear."

The lips of the beautiful girl parted, but no sound came from them.

She was too startled, too terrified to speak.

Fear froze the words in her mouth.

A peculiar smile flitted over the pirate's face as he unclasped his teeth and withdrew the pipe he had commenced to smoke with so much complacency.

"Come, come, my sweet dove," he said, with a merry twinkle in his eyes, "be not alarmed; surely there is nothing so terrible in me. I am only Captain Kydd"

And darting forward he seized Violet rudely by her wrist.

"Help! help! help!" she screamed, struggling vainly with him.

"It is at hand," cried the voice which had so startled and mystified captain and crew alike. "I am Lionel-of-the-Sea."

And as he gave utterance to these words our boy hero climbed over the side of the vessel.

The next instant his feet were planted firmly on the deck.

Down went a man who endeavoured to stay the lad's progress.

The pirates taken by surprise, rushed hither and thither in confusion, save a few who kept their senses about them and prepared to repel boarders.

Captain Kydd released Violet's arm from his iron grasp, and stood speechless with amazement and white with fury.

As he rushed forward, sword in hand, to meet Lionel, the spectre of Vanderdecken appeared.

"You here?" Captain Kydd hissed.

"Yes," Vanderdecken replied, "to help the good and shield the helpless. Beware! It is not too late to repent."

The mysterious form vanished as quickly and sharply as it had appeared.

By this time Lionel-of-the-Sea had reached Violet, and was supporting her half-fainting form.

Captain Kydd made a signal to his men, and a rush was made in Lionel's direction.

Our hero drew himself up with proud defiance, and clapped the muzzle of his pistol against one of the powder kegs.

"Back, Captain Kydd!" cried Lionel-of-the-Sea, "or by the sun that is shining down upon us I will involve this ship and all that she contains in one common and instantaneous destruction. I have but to bend my finger, and bolts of red sulphur will split the Vampire's ribs, and hurl every living creature she contains high into the skies."

A MUTTERED imprecation fell from Kydd's lips.

The fierce and scowling pirates might have been so many idiotic picturesque statues, so motionless did they stand.

They were awe-stricken at the mysterious manner in which Lionel came on board.

There was a silence, broken only by the flapping of the sails, the creaking of the timbers, and the straining of the cords, as the Vampire, with unabated speed, ploughed her way through the foam-crested waves.

"Are you going to obey me, or am I to fire?" demanded our hero. "Unhand the lady this instant!"

Captain Kydd relaxed his grasp, and reluctantly took his hand from Violet's arm.

Full well did the pirate captain know that Lionel-of-the-Sea would be as good as his word.

That the boy would, without any hesitation, carry out his threat Nero and all the others were equally well aware.

Violet Everleigh gave vent to an exclamation of joy, and, rushing to the side of the cask, sank down upon her knees.

"Saved!"

That was the word she gasped as our hero coolly seated himself on the keg.

Baffled and bewildered, the thwarted pirate glared at our hero like a tiger despoiled of his prey.

"The first one who moves hand or foot without my permission gives the signal for me to fire. Remember Lionel-of-the-Sea never breaks his word."

"Death and destruction!" growled Captain Kydd.

"Swear away," said Lionel, with a smile of scorn. "Bad language will neither frighten me nor change the aspect of affairs. I am master of the situation."

"Curse you!" howled Kydd, fairly foaming at the mouth.

"That's it. Proceed."

"Death and the devil!"

"Invoke not those two angels, for neither of them do you wish to see."

"Bitterly shall you rue this insolence, boy. Heartily shall you regret this folly. Yours is only a momentary triumph; my time will come!"

"Possibly," was the cool reply; "but I command here now, and intend to steer for Table Bay at once. What is your name?"

This latter question he addressed to the fair girl who crouched at his feet.

"Violet!" gasped our heroine.

"Well, Violet, you are a brave girl, I know. Will you help me to retain my position?"

"Oh, yes, indeed I will."

And rising to her feet, beside the keg, she glanced proudly and defiantly, first at Captain Kydd, secondly at Nero, and thirdly into the menacing visages of the pirate horde.

"Good!" exclaimed our hero, approvingly. "Now, Captain Kydd, listen to me. It is true that we are some four days' sail from Table Bay, but since there are two of us it will be easy to keep this pistol directed at the barrel the whole time. When I want a few hours' repose my fair companion will prove herself as resolute as I am. If at any time either you or any of your blood-thirsty wretches venture to approach within a certain distance without permission your vessel will be blown up. I think you pretty clearly understand the exact position of affairs."

Captain Kydd ground his teeth, but made no

reply.

"Now I am going to issue my commands."

"One moment," interrupted Violet.

"What is it?" cried our hero.

"I have an idea."

Our hero stared at her with surprise and admiration.

"An idea!" he echoed. "Well, what is it?"

"It is to materially strengthen our position."

"In what way?"

"There is on board a prisoner, a brave young Dutchman, the son of the captain of the Zuyder Zee."

"Well, and what of that?"

"He fought for me like a lion when the pirates attacked us, and is, I am sure, as valiant and chivalric as yourself."

"Ah! I see. You think he will be a valuable acquisition?"

Voilet's cheeks flushed.

"I'm sure of it," she said.

"Then we will have him," said our hero. "What is his name?"

"Hans Van Ryder."

"Captain Kydd," cried our hero, "you have a prisoner, one Hans Van Ryder. Liberate him instantly. Supply him with a brace of pistols and a cutlass, and send him here forthwith. This is my first command. Obey it promptly, or I keep my threat."

It was something fearful to hear how the pirate cursed and swore; but all to no avail. He knew the utter helplessness of his position.

There was fearful danger even in a moment's hesitation.

Beckoning Nero to follow him, he stalked forward in solemn silence.

The equally perplexed and furious black hastened after him.

Then the two disappeared down the main hatchway.

A brief interval elapsed.

During this time not a word was spoken on the Vampire's deck.

Then the young Dutchman, looking somewhat pale and haggard, emerged from the hatchway, grasping a cutlass in one hand and a very formidable double-barrelled pistol in the other.

After him came Captain Kydd and Nero.

Hans Van Ryder looked around him with a somewhat puzzled air.

But his eyes quickly found what they sought.

That was Violet Everleigh.

The moment he saw her the young Dutchman broke into a run.

He reached the spot occupied by our hero with a bound.

Hans regarded Lionel with a searching gaze, and then looked at Violet inquiringly.

"Oh, Hans!" exclaimed the latter, "is not this a terrible situation?"

"It is, indeed, and, what is still worse, I fear we shall never escape from it."

"No! no! Do not say so! We must have courage, Hans, and hope for the best."

"Oh, yes, we must do that."

"There is One above, Hans, without whose consent our destruction cannot be effected. In this hour of supreme trial let us put our trust in Him, and school ourselves to believe that all which happens will be for the best. Rest assured He has some wise purpose to accomplish, or all these things could not take place."

"Heaven bless you for those words—those noble sentiments, Violet!" cried Hans, with sparkling eyes. "But tell me how it is that I have been set free and armed?"

"It means," replied our hero, "that things have taken a turn for the better. All now depends upon our own vigilance and firmness. At present we are virtually commanders of this ship."

"Nonsense!"

"A fact, I assure you. We are, at least, in a position to issue orders and to enforce their fulfilment."

"Explain."

Lionel-of-the-Sea told Hans Van Ryder exactly how matters stood.

The young Dutchman was astounded.

Nevertheless, he was quick enough to perceive that the position which our hero had taken up was, indeed, a very strong one.

"But who are you, and how came you here? You did not belong to the Queen of the Zuyder Zee."

"Ah! I did not think of asking that question," cried Violet, turning her great hazel eyes upon our hero with wondering admiration.

"I am Lionel-of-the-Sea," replied our hero; "but how I came to be here at this moment I must for the present decline to tell. Be satisfied with the knowledge that I arrived at a most opportune moment for both of you, and that Captain Kydd knows for certain that when I threaten to blow the Vampire up unless my orders are obeyed I shall be as good as my word."

"Look! that dreadful black man is approaching," cried Violet.

As she spoke Nero came lounging slowly towards them.

The black lieutenant had removed from his person the traces of a recent fight with a little water and by changing his shirt.

Nero always wore the whitest and finest linen that could possibly be procured.

Like Richard the Third this brawny butcher was a perfect dandy.

"Advance!" cried Lionel, in a voice of command.

He held his pistols threateningly as he spoke.

Nero came forward a few paces.

"Halt!" He stopped.

The black lieutenant of the Vampire knew that had he refused to obey our hero's order the total destruction of the ship and all on board would immediately ensue.

His great eyes gleamed malignantly and his lips curled and quivered with the rage that was consuming him.

"Half a dozen bottles of wine," cried Lionel, as if he had been addressing the waiter at an hostelrie. "A cask of the best biscuits and a good cheese."

Nero stared at him in sullen defiance.

"Begone! do my bidding! or——"

The black moved discontentedly away.

Shortly afterwards the articles were brought by a trio of ill-favoured rascals, and placed on the spot indicated by our hero.

They were about to depart when Lionel called out to them.

"Hi! stop! A cask of water and two bottles of brandy."

These articles were fetched and placed with the other stores.

"Now tell Captain Kydd that Lionel-of-the-Sea wishes to consult him."

"You wish to consult with me," remarked Captain Kydd, with a haughty look.

"Yes," replied Lionel-of-the-Sea. "I want to know which course you deem it advisable to pursue—from here to the sky, and from the sky to the bottom of the sea, in charred and blackened fragments, or from here to Table Bay direct?"

Captain Kydd gnashed his teeth with rage.

His brow grew black as a thunder-cloud.

For a moment the fate of all trembled in the balance.

The crew drew closer and looked on in breathless suspense.

The pirates knew their captain's desperate nature, and were fearful lest, in the heat of his rage, he should choose the most desperate of the two alternatives offered by our hero.

Our hero was equally well aware that there was some likelihood of this, and therefore prepared himself for the supreme moment.

He was resolved that, should it be necessary, he would unfalteringly put his threat into execution.

"Well," he inquired of Captain Kydd, "which way is it to be—this or that?"

He first pointed over the water and then up at the sky with much significance.

"For the present," replied the pirate captain, "we steer towards Cape Town."

"A wise decision, Captain Kydd."

"So I think," muttered the pirate; "for if I don't manage to turn the tables upon you before you are twenty-four hours older I'll submit to be keel-hauled. Nero!"

"Yes, captain," answered Nero, to the summons of Captain Kydd.

"Come with me."

And turning on his heel he walked aft to the state cabin.

It was a most elegant and luxurious place.

Nero followed him in and closed the door.

Captain Kydd flung himself upon one of the rich crimson velvet ottomans, and writhing about in mortal agony, poured forth the most horrible imprecations that were ever strung together.

The utterance of these frightful sentences seemed to give some ease to the pirate's troubled heart, for presently he became comparatively cool, and began to smoke a Turkish hookah.

"Now, what is to be done?"

"I cannot think; we are in a most disagreeable position. Fancy that young cub turning up again; thought he was fathoms deep beneath

the surface of the waves."

"Curse him! He seems to have as many lives as a cat. But how did he get on board?"

"Some one must have helped him; there is a traitor on the Vampire."

"I hardly think that that can be, Nero. No, no; there is some mystery about all this which neither you nor I can fathom yet. But I will fathom it before long. In the meantime we must confine ourselves to one question alone—that is, how to change the aspect of affairs on deck."

"Yes. Have you nothing to suggest?"

"Nothing. You see the young devil cannot be approached with safety while he is on that barrel; and now he has that infernal young Dutchman to help him. Nothing can be easier than for them to retain their position until the Revenge shows up, or the Cape is reached."

"Death and fury!"

"You see, so long as they keep guard over the keg, and the keg is full of powder——"

Captain Kydd gave vent to an abrupt exclamation, and leapt to his feet.

Nero, thus rudely interrupted, stared in amazement at the pirate.

Captain Kydd clapped his hands, and laughed loudly.

Had he suddenly taken leave of his senses?

It looked very much like it.

"Ha—ha—ha!" laughed Captain Kydd. "I have it—I have it."

"Have what?" asked Nero, still more puzzled than ever.

"The idea, Nero—the idea. Oh, it is a capital one. Ha—ha—ha! Captain Kydd will yet win the game."

The face of the black lieutenant instantly lit up.

"Good," he cried. "And what, Captain Kydd, is this idea by which we shall be able to outwit Lionel and obtain possession of the girl, who seemingly is named Violet?"

"Oh, it is an extremely simple one. Where is the carpenter?"

"The carpenter!"

"Yes; you are right, Nero, when you say that so long as there is powder in the keg Lionel can set us at defiance. But why is there powder in the keg?"

"Because it has been put there, I suppose," replied the negro.

"But that is no reason why it should remain. Ha! ha! I think we shall astonish Master Lionel, after all."

CHAPTER VII.

THE PIRATE'S TRIUMPH.

"You propose to extract the powder from the cask by some secret means?" said Nero, inquiringly.

"Most decidedly," rejoined Captain Kydd.

"But I must confess I am baffled in my attempt to guess the means by which you intend to accomplish your object.

"Ha! ha! Why nothing can be more simple. All we have to do is to set the carpenter at work immediately beneath the barrel. He can cut through the deck without the slightest noise, make a hole in the bottom of the cask, and then down will come the powder, which must be caught in an empty keg, and then removed in case of accidents. Do you not see it all now?"

"As clearly as in a mirror," replied the delighted negro, with a chuckle of delight, as he rubbed his great hands together. "The idea is worthy of you, Captain Kydd; it is a most excellent one."

"Then we will lose no time in carrying it out."

Then the carpenter was sent for and instructed.

The three then proceeded to the poop-cabin.

The chief difficulty was to hit upon the exact spot on which the powder-keg stood.

This, however, the carpenter disposed of in a professional manner, and then set to work with a will.

Kydd and Nero watched him with no little anxiety.

Gleams of satisfaction shot from time to time from their eyes.

Little did our hero suspect what was going on beneath him.

The carpenter's tools were of the very best description, and in a very short time he had made a hole sufficiently large for the purpose.

Over this was the bottom of the powder keg.

He had now to proceed with greater caution.

It was highly necessary that the bottom of the keg should be cut away so gently that our hero, who sat on the top, should not feel the slightest shock.

This the pirate-carpenter succeeded in doing with no little exercise of skill.

Then down with a run came the black stream of powder.

The empty keg, which had been procured on purpose to receive it, was instantly placed in such a position that every grain of powder fell into it.

Captain Kydd chuckled gleefully.

Nero placed his hands to his sides and rolled and twisted about as if convulsed with restrained laughter.

But neither ventured to give full vent to their feelings.

To have done so would have been highly imprudent.

If Lionel had heard them his suspicions would immediately have been aroused, and their little game spoilt.

Not until every atom of the powder had fallen through the hole did Captain Kydd and Nero quit the poop-cabin.

Nero and the carpenter carried the powder away between them, and stowed it for safety in the magazine.

"Now then, Nero," shouted Kydd, "come on, I shall require your assistance; and, besides, you ought not to miss a bit of fun."

"All right, captain," replied that worthy.

Then the two made their way to the poop.

Here Lionel was perched as boldly as ever, and he regarded the two pirates with an air of conscious power.

Hans Van Ryder stood by his side.

Violet Everleigh was reclining, upon one of the bales, which Hans Van Ryder had pushed close to the powder keg for her convenience.

"Halt!" cried Lionel-of-the-Sea, the moment he considered that Kydd and Nero had advanced as close as was requisite for all honest purposes. "Halt, or I fire."

It was with the utmost difficulty that Nero prevented himself from arousing our hero's suspicion that all was not well, by the expression of his features.

He, however, half-averted his face, and pretended to be gazing intently seawards.

Captain Kydd, however, was a consummate actor.

"Now then, Lionel," he said, in an off-hand manner, "what's the good of carrying on such a ridiculous warfare as this? You know what sort of man I am. We are now sailing in the direction of Table Bay, but I need not inform you that Captain Kydd would rather blow the ship up with his own hand than allow himself to be taken even by such a frigate as the Revenge, and therefore it is absurd to suppose he would permit two boys and a girl to sail him and the whole of his crew into a port where he would be instantly seized. No, no, my lad. Either you or I shall apply a light to the gunpowder first; but we have at least four days before us, and I hope we shall be able to come to some sort of understanding before we are driven to so extreme a course."

"Well?"

"Well, I'll take you to any of the islands along the coast which are frequented by traders, and where you would be sure to be picked up before long, and leave you there in peace and safety. What do you say to that?"

"Why, then, Captain Kydd, if I could depend upon your word, I would accept the offer at once; but you have no more regard for the most solemn oath or promise than for a merchant's throat, and, auguring from the past, I know full well that you would promise anything, and then, the moment I had fulfilled my part of the contract, you would ruthlessly break yours, and we should all three be at your mercy."

"Pooh! I seek for no revenge now. Accept my offer, and you may go in peace. If you like, you can go at once. The longboat, well stored, is entirely at your service, and not only are ships constantly passing and repassing here, but the Revenge is actually on our track, and any minute may appear upon the scene."

Lionel-of-the-Sea whispered to Hans.

The young Dutchman replied.

A consultation in a low voice was carried on between them.

Nero and Captain Kydd, without appearing to do so, eagerly watched their movements.

"Well," inquired the captain, "what decision have you arrived at?"

"Captain Kydd, we doubt your word, and therefore decline your offer."

"Now then, boys, seize them!" cried Kydd, suddenly altering his tone and manner, as he pointed to the two with his cutlass.

"Ha! what means this?" exclaimed Lionel, hurriedly. "The time has come, then. Farewell, Hans! Farewell, Violet! We will all die together, and accomplish a glorious end by our death—the destruction of the Vampire and her fiendish crew."

Bang!

With steady hand Lionel-of-the-Sea fired his pistol into the keg.

There was a peal of laughter from Captain Kydd and Nero.

A rush of feet.

Hans and Lionel were instantly seized by a score of sinewy hands.

Then, with a shout of triumph, Captain Kydd sprang forward and caught Violet up in his arms.

CHAPTER VIII.

FURTHER SURPRISES—CAPTAIN KYDD IS PERFECTLY BEWILDERED.

VIOLET shrieked in wild despair as the pirate threw his strong arms round her form.

Lionel-of-the-Sea seemed petrified with amazement.

So did Hans Van Ryder.

The two heroic lads had fully prepared themselves for the blaze and roar of the explosion which was to hurl their shattered bodies high up into the air, and scatter their limbs in all directions.

Lionel, still holding the pistol, from the muzzle of which the smoke came curling upwards, looked at the powder keg in blank amazement.

What was the meaning of it?

As yet not the faintest suspicion of the truth crossed his mind.

Hans Van Ryder was literally thunderstruck.

A mocking and triumphant laugh came from Captain Kydd as he hastened to the state cabin with Violet, even though struggling and shrieking in his arms.

The pirate crew now gathered round the two boys.

"Hans Van Ryder," cried Lionel-of-the-Sea, as pale as death, yet with fierce aspect and unquavering voice, "place your back to mine. The odds against us are overwhelming, but at least we will not die alone."

Quick as thought the young Dutchman turned his back to our hero's.

Thus stood the two dauntless boys, sword and pistol in hand, while the crew of fierce pirates which hemmed them in came closer and closer each moment.

With a hideous grin and low chuckle of satisfaction Nero stood forward a pace.

"Ha, ha! my young cockerels," he said, making a horrible facial contortion; "clever as you deem yourselves, you see Captain Kydd has outdone you after all. He's in his element now. Ha, ha, ha! Just listen for a moment. There's a pleasant requiem for you."

Louder and still more shrill Violet's shrieks pealed through the ship.

Lionel could endure it no longer.

He would bring matters to a crisis.

With amazing rapidity he altered the direction of his pistol.

There was a flash and a bang.

Nero uttered a yell like a wild beast, and staggered back.

Then there was another report, and another howl.

Hans Van Ryder had fired his pistol also, and a fierce, half Spanish-looking miscreant spun round once, and fell.

The young Dutchman had shot him through the heart.

The enraged pirates dashed forward, and the two gallant lads, after a severe struggle, were disarmed and held fast.

Yells of gratification came from the ferocious crew of the Vampire, and Nero, who looked more frightful than ever, owing to the fact that his head had been roughly bandaged with a handkerchief, drawing his kreese, advanced towards the two boys in a crouching posture.

The keen, bright, jagged weapon glistened in the air just over our hero's form!

Another instant and it would have been buried to the hilt in Lionel's heart!

But, by one of those extraordinary interventions of Providence, the negro's arm was arrested in its descent.

A wild cry of amazement and terror burst from the lips of the crew.

Nero started and glanced around.

"What is it?" he asked.

The eyes of the pirates were all turned in one direction, and every visage was blanched or distorted with fear.

Nero looked to see what it was, and then, uttering a yell, he sprang to an upright position, and gazed with starting eyeballs at the object which had spread such universal dismay throughout the pirate ship.

"Hullo! What's up now? What means all this uproar?" demanded a loud voice.

And Captain Kydd, looking very hot and excited, rushed through the gangway with a pistol in his hand.

"Look, look!" gasped Nero. "It is the Flying Dutchman!"

As he spoke, the negro lieutenant of the Vampire pointed with his kreese to leeward.

A phantom ship, under a perfect cloud of white and vapourish-looking canvas, was flying past at a truly miraculous speed.

A frightful imprecation broke from Captain Kydd's lips.

"Death and destruction!" he roared. "If she was only a little nearer I'd treat her to a broadside. Phantom or no phantom, I'd blow her clean out of the water."

There was no doubt but that Captain Kydd was in earnest.

And now, by one of those powerful and almost superhuman efforts, of which he was capable at times, the celebrated pirate recovered his presence of mind.

"Nero," he cried, with bated breath, "I'll do what no other sea-captain has ever dared to do since the Flying Dutchman has been beating about the Cape. I'll send a shot from the bow-chaser smashing through the phantom's hull, be the consequences what they may. This way!"

And with hasty steps he made his way to the fore.

With Nero's aid the bow-chaser was run out.

Captain Kydd directed it himself.

The celebrated pirate was an unerring marksman.

Boom!

There was a dull and sullen roar.

A puff of smoke.

Captain Kydd and Nero strained their eyes to note the effect of the shot.

Overawed and speechless, the crew did likewise.

A grim smile appeared on the face of the celebrated pirate.

"Can you see her, Nero?"

"No."

The Flying Dutchman was gone.

The phantom ship had vanished.

Captain Kydd swept the horizon with his glass. But no sign or trace of any vessel did he see.

"Ha! ha! ha!" laughed Captain Kydd, making his way aft again, with a swaggering smile. "The pirate laughs at all dangers, scoffs at all foes, and conquers everywhere. But, stay; those boys must die."

And he stepped up to the spot where lay our hero and the young Dutchman, now bound with cords.

Lionel-of-the-Sea moved restlessly.

Then he, with an evident effort, raised himself up on one arm, and, passing his hand before his eyes, as if to clear away some mist that hovered before them, he gazed dreamily around.

With a growl of fury Nero again unsheathed his kreese, and, with a panther-like step, advanced towards our hero.

"Back!" cried Captain Kydd, motioning Nero to stop, with a commanding gesture. "Death would be too good a fate for either of them."

But even the dreaded Nero dared not disobey Captain Kydd.

Indeed, he had to conceal his disapproval to the best of his ability.

"Now, then, some of you there, look sharp. Bring irons for two, and clap these youngsters into the second cabin, for, by Jupiter, I mean to sell them both for slaves."

"Slaves!" echoed Lionel, bitterly. "Slaves! Ha—ha!"

But though our hero's heart was stout enough his voice and laugh had a very dismal and dissonant sound.

"Away with them!" cried Kydd.

A dozen eager hands clutched our hero and his companion.

A few minutes after they were ironed our hero's head dropped upon his breast, and Hans, rolling over on his side, fell into a death-like stupor.

Though Lionel's eyes were heavy and his thoughts confused, he was not asleep.

He became conscious that Vanderdecken was present, and, more wonderful still, that the irons which had been placed upon his limbs were lying at his feet.

Then, still half-dreaming, he found himself walking at the spectre's side.

"Blame me not for what has happened," Vanderdecken said, "there are some things which are beyond my power at present, but fear not, my triumph and your's will come in good time. It is ordained that you must remain a prisoner and suffer, but be of good heart."

"I care not for myself," Lionel said, "only rescue Violet. She is too young and beautiful to remain here."

Vanderdecken smiled as he raised, slapped, and waved his hands above Lionel's head.

Our hero started, and not without good reason.

The scene had changed, and he was in Captain Kydd's cabin.

Violet fast asleep was reposing on a couch and Vanderdecken was gazing down upon her with a pitying glance.

"Touch her not, nor attempt to awaken her," Vanderdecken said; "I have brought you here to show you that she lives, and I protected her from her enemies. Back!"

The spectre uttered this last word as if addressing somebody near him, and Lionel felt his senses reel.

When he came to himself he found that Hans Van Ryder was at his side, and nothing had been changed.

"So," Lionel said, "it was nothing but a dream after all."

He glanced down at the irons and sighed.

"Have you lost courage?" said a voice; "have you lost confidence in me so soon?"

It was the voice of Vanderdecken.

Once more let us return to the deck of the Vampire.

Captain Kydd paced up and down in gloomy silence.

He had conquered. Lionel-of-the-Sea and Hans Van Ryder were in his power, but the pirate was ill at ease.

An air of mystery hung about the vessel.

The wind had dropped suddenly, and a mist of leaden hue darkened sky and sea.

It was like the hush and awful stillness that precedes the bursting of a terrific thunderstorm.

The crew of the Vampire were on the look out, for at any moment the elements might be in conflict.

Suddenly Captain Kydd stopped, and called Nero to his side.

"I wish to speak to the young Dutchman alone," the pirate said. "See that his irons are removed, and take him to your own cabin.

Nero looked surprised.

For a moment he thought that Captain Kydd was going out of his mind.

"Will it be safe to do so," the black lieutenant asked. "Hans Van Ryder is as strong as he is brave. Give him the freedom of his limbs, and I would not care to answer for the consequences."

"Do as I tell you," Captain Kydd said, frowning. "I have some questions to ask him, and should he answer them I may be inclined to offer him his liberty."

Nero shrugged his shoulders as he called two men.

They went below, and in a few minutes the black lieutenant reappeared on deck.

"Your order has been obeyed," he said. "Hans Van Ryder is in my cabin."

"That is well," Captain Kydd said. "Keep within call, for—— Bah! why should I fear him when I am armed?"

The pirate chief found Hans Van Ryder reclining full length upon a couch.

"I am glad to see that you have made yourself at home," Captain Kydd said, smiling grimly as he closed the door.

"Certainly," Hans said. "It is my disposition to make myself as comfortable as possible. Why have you brought me here?"

"To question you concerning Violet. Who is she?"

"You want to know the history of her birth and parentage?"

"Yes."

"Then," said Hans, "you had better ask her yourself."

"Beware!" Captain Kydd said, scowling savagely. "You forget that you are in my power."

"I forget nothing," Hans replied, calmly, "not even that you are the greatest scoundrel who has as yet escaped the gallows."

"Listen to the voice of reason," said the pirate chief. "You are young, and life has many charms for you. Tell me what I want to know, and instead of dooming you to slavery I will set you free, and load you with presents such as a prince would be proud to possess."

"I scorn your offers as I laugh at your threats," Hans replied. "I should be a cur indeed if I gave your words a single thought."

"Then, by the darkness of Hades, I will give you your liberty, for you shall die."

As Captain Kydd hissed out these words he drew a long shining dagger and advanced towards Hans.

In an instant an icy hand was upon his throat, an iron grasp upon the hand that held the dagger, and Captain Kydd shrieked aloud as he saw that he was being held by Vanderdecken.

The spectre's appearance was so sudden and awful that Hans uttered a cry of alarm, and almost swooned.

"Help!" Captain Kydd shouted. "Help! Nero, come to my rescue!"

The black lieutenant, followed by two of the crew, burst into the cabin.

They found the pirate chief writhing on the ground, as if in the agonies of death.

"How now?" Nero demanded. "What is the meaning of this?"

"Secure the prisoner, and take him back to the hold," Captain Kydd gasped. "I have seen Vanderdecken. His death-like clutch has been upon me."

"Nonsense," Nero said; "you have been drinking heavily. Come, Hans, you must go back

to your companion, though, had I my will, I would separate you with a vengeance."

Captain Kydd saw Hans dragged away, and then, after bracing his nerves with a deep draught of brandy, went to his own cabin.

Captain Kydd glanced swiftly round.

But where was Violet?

No trace of her could he see.

Nevertheless, Captain Kydd felt quite sure that she must be hiding somewhere in the cabin, for, on quitting it, he had left her in a half-senseless state, huddled up on the floor.

And he had taken great care to securely lock the door of the cabin afterwards.

"Come, come," cried Captain Kydd, "'tis useless to hide. Show yourself at once, or it will be worse for you."

Then he commenced a thorough search of the cabin.

Neither nook nor corner escaped him.

He overturned all the ottomans, upset all the furniture. He looked all over the sleeping apartment beyond.

But without the least success.

Violet Everleigh had gone.

The renowned pirate actually went black in the face with passion.

Glaring round him like a wild bull, he picked up a large pistol, the butt of which was heavily mounted with brass.

With this he banged furiously at a gong; nor did he cease till some one tapped at the door.

"Come in," roared Kydd.

"I can't," replied the deep bass voice of his sable lieutenant. "The door is locked."

In the heat of his passion Captain Kydd had quite forgotten this circumstance.

With impatient movement he threw the door wide open.

With his head still bandaged up, and his fingers stuck idly in his sash, Nero sauntered in, "Where's the girl?"

And lightning seemed to dart and gleam from his eyes as he fixed them upon the negro.

"The girl, captain," replied Nero. "I know nothing of the girl. I thought she was in here with you. To my certain knowledge no one has been near your cabin-door since you left it yourself. I presume you locked it when you came on deck."

"I did, but she is gone."

Nero shrugged his shoulders.

"Mayhaps the devil's flown away with her."

"The devil be hanged. He'd as leave touch holy water. I tell you she is somewhere near at hand, and therefore must be found. Look, you, Nero. I've made up my mind to love that girl, and the Father of Evil himself shall not thwart me. Look!"

The negro looked into his captain's face, and saw how terribly in earnest he was.

But he spoke not.

"Now," said Captain Kydd, with an imperious gesture, "go and tell the crew what I have said, and see that the Vampire is searched from keel to masthead."

Nero bowed himself out of the cabin.

The negro knew very well that it would not do to trifle with Captain Kydd in his present humour.

He saw that the pirate's orders were carried out to the very letter.

The hold was ransacked, the store-room invaded, every berth was visited, every corner peered into ; in short, not a hole big enough for a mouse to creep in was left unprobed.

But all in vain.

The confusion and uproar that ensued defies description.

Ominous whispers circulated rapidly amongst the crew.

CHAPTER X.

A STRUGGLE FOR LIBERTY — VANDERDECKEN APPEARS AGAIN—OUR HERO AND HIS FRIEND HANS FIND THEMSELVES IN A SAD PLIGHT.

LIKE all sailors, Captain Kydd's lawless crew were exceedingly superstitious. Therefore they liked not the sudden disappearance of the lovely Violet Everleigh.

The storm that raged within the pirate's heart seemed as if it were never going to abate.

He cursed, he swore, he tore his hair, and occasionally dealt heavy blows with his fist at some of the men without any cause whatever.

In fine, the celebrated pirate raved like an unchained madman for more than four hours.

And even when he sank back with a groan upon an ottoman, utterly and entirely exhausted, his livid flesh quivered with rage.

He placed a small silver whistle to his lips, and blew a clear blast thereon.

This was a signal for his boy Pedro to appear before him.

The youth entered.

He was a tall, slim, elegant fellow, of about seventeen, attired in that very elegant costume adopted by Spanish caballeros of the seventeenth century.

"A goblet of madeira, Pedro."

The youth threw open a cupboard, in which was a splendid array of Venetian glass, and poured out a goblet of luscious wine.

This Captain Kydd drained to the dregs.

"That will do, boy. Now send Nero to me once more."

The boy bowed gracefully and departed.

Captain Kydd lit his very elegant hookah, and smoked thoughtfully until Nero made his appearance.

The negro eyed him askant.

"Any sign of the Revenge?"

"No, captain," replied Nero. "She seems to have lost scent of us."

"And a good job, too," cried Kydd, heartily, "but I'm afraid she will bore us yet, terribly. Your English blue-jacket is by no means so easily disheartened. Well, how far are we from the island of Dileloe?"

"We shall sight it in two hours. But do you mean to put in there?"

"Most certainly," replied Kydd, coolly.

"But King Bangalibaleo," suggested Nero.

"What of him?" asked Kydd, with a quiet smile.

And he blew another cloud from his pipe.

"Well, you remember that last transaction ?" said Nero. "Surely that cannot have faded from your memory ? It occurs to me that his majesty will be inclined to act very unkindly towards you this time."

Captain Kydd laughed.

"That's an insinuation, Nero. I don't think Bangalibaleo is a man who indulges in private prejudices. And, furthermore, Nero, the Vampire's guns will carry into the very centre of the slave market, and further than that I do not intend to proceed. If his majesty shows the least coolness I shall give a signal. You will be on board the Vampire, and will know how to respond to it. But sell those boys I will, and at once."

"But——" began Nero, when he was interrupted by a knock at the door.

"Come in," cried Captain Kydd.

A fierce-looking Malay entered.

"What is it?" demanded the pirate captain.

"Land!" laconically replied the Malay.

And turning on his heel he unceremoniously returned to the deck.

The pirate captain sprang to his feet.

"It must be Dileloe," said Nero. "Do we sail into the bay at once ?"

"Certainly," replied Kydd. "You can give the necessary orders. I am going to interview young Lionel."

Nero bowed and quitted the cabin.

Captain Kydd made his way to that part of the hold where the two prisoners were confined.

He found Lionel and Hans Van Ryder sitting up and conversing in a low tone.

They ceased speaking the moment that Kydd appeared on the scene.

"Well, my boys," commenced the pirate captain, in a jocular manner, "I've come to congratulate you upon your trappings."

Hans gave a grunt of disgust.

"Well, then," continued Kydd, "as you like. Then we'll say to commiserate with your present misfortunes. You shall find me a veritable Job's comforter. I've no doubt you find this hold very close and stifling ; and I know it is awfully monotonous to sit in the dark with a quarter-of-a hundredweight of iron attached to one's limbs. What do you say to a pleasant little trip ashore ?"

Hans pricked up his ears.

Lionel-of-the-Sea, however, who knew Captain Kydd of old, darted him a glance of defiance.

"The Island of Dileloe is a most salubrious spot—an earthly Paradise—a perfect little Eden— and there's such a nice slave-market hard by the shore ; and, as you have been such good boys, I mean to let you see it."

"The sooner the better," Lionel said. "You are the greatest scoundrel on the face of the earth, and the sooner that I know that I am well out of your sight the better I shall like it."

Captain Kydd frowned until his bushy eyebrows met.

"I cannot help admiring your pluck," he said. "You are too young to die; will you recant and become one of my crew?"

"If I am too young to die," Lionel replied, boldly, "I am old enough to know the iniquity of giving myself up to a villanous life. I scorn you and your offer. Do your worst."

"What do you say?" Captain Kydd demanded, turning to Hans Van Ryder.

"That Lionel's sentiments are mine," Hans replied. "Listen, pirate and hang-dog. Long before I met you face to face, and saw my father slain by your bloodthirsty hirelings, I heard of you. You are the fiend in human shape who slays children and unoffending women. Your greed for gold and love of cruelty are well known, and your name stinks in the nostrils of all brave and honest men."

"Bravo, Hans!" Lionel-of-the-Sea cried, "that is the way to tackle him. See how the villain quails under your eye."

Captain Kydd folded his arms and laughed hoarsely.

"Hans Van Ryder," he said, "I shall have the opportunity of trying your Dutch courage presently."

"You will find some true metal in it," Hans replied, boldly.

Captain Kydd laid his hand upon his sword, and half unsheathed it.

"Bah!" he said, as he returned the weapon with a clang. "Why should I trouble myself about a pair of whelps?"

"You would not dare to call us by that name if we were free," Lionel said. "If you did not fear us you would bid us go, but you are a base coward at heart."

Captain Kydd bit his under lip till blood flowed and ran down his chin.

His face grew livid as his eyes glowed with a baneful light.

Suddenly he turned and strode out of the hold.

"What a villain he is," Lionel said. "Oh, for an hour of freedom. Oh for a cutlass and a fair chance to conquer or perish."

Our hero spoke passionately, and as he moved restlessly something fell with a ringing sound at his feet.

It was a file of the finest steel.

"Here's a stroke of luck," our hero cried joyfully. "No gift from Heaven could be more welcome just now. Now Hans, my boy, sit still, and I will soon file your irons through."

"No," said the young Dutchman; "attend to yourself first."

"That I refuse to do," Lionel replied. "I would sooner throw the file beyond my reach."

Finding that Lionel-of-the-Sea was determined to have his way, Hans Van Ryder said no more, and our hero went to work with a will.

One by one the irons fell from Hans, and presently he stood erect, and breathing a sigh of relief, stretched himself.

"Now," said Lionel, who was perspiring from the exertions he had undergone, "you may do

the like for me. Be quick about it, or Captain Kydd may take it into his head to return."

In a very few minutes Lionel-of-the-Sea was free.

"Now follow me," he whispered. "We must go to the armoury and secure weapons at any cost. Hist! What is that?"

Footsteps sounded above head, but they died away quickly, and the two boys, after crouching down a few seconds and listening intently, began to creep through the hold.

It was a journey fraught with danger.

The appearance of a single man might upset their plans, and they knew that they carried their lives in their hands.

The dead lights shone with a fitful glare upon them, but at last they began to ascend, and presently came to a number of cutlasses ranged in the form of a star.

Lionel-of-the-Sea and Hans Van Ryder armed themselves, and stood ready for any emergency.

At this moment Nero, Captain Kydd's black lieutenant, appeared on deck.

At a glance he saw how matters stood, and his swarthy face became convulsed with rage.

His stentorious voice sounded the alarm, but he had reason to repent of having done so.

Hans Van Ryder sent a bullet after him with such good aim that Nero fell wounded in the left shoulder.

Yelling with pain and cursing the brave boys, he scrambled to his feet, and making his way down the ladder soon roused the fiendish crew.

On came Captain Kydd and his villanous gang.

"Cut them down, but do not kill them," the pirate chief shouted. "I have a fate worse than death in store for them."

Such a defence as theirs could not last long.

They fought long and gallantly, but at last their cutlasses were beaten out of their hands.

To have offered any resistance now would simply have been absurd

This both the boys knew perfectly well.

Therefore they staggered to their feet and reeled rather than walked in the footsteps of Captain Kydd.

Both were fearfully faint.

Indeed, the loss of blood they had sustained was something serious.

With a naked cutlass in his hand the smith brought up the rear.

As he crossed the deck Lionel reeled and almost fell.

Never before had he felt so sick, so faint, so dizzy!

Sky, sea, and deck seemed to swim around him.

A blood-red mist hung like a curtain before his eyes.

It was only by a very great effort our hero was enabled to maintain his balance.

With uncertain steps, like those of a drunken man, Lionel—half unconscious of where he was, and wholly indifferent as to what was going on around him—made his way to the lee bulwarks, against which he was glad to prop himself.

Hans Van Ryder was almost equally as exhausted.

"Water!" gasped Lionel. "Give me water!"

"Brandy!" cried Captain Kydd. "That's the sort of stuff he wants."

Some very fine cognac was instantly brought by Pedro.

Our hero drank it greedily.

The effect of the spirits upon him was truly wonderful!

Indeed, it revived him so much, that in les than a minute he was able to stand without su[port and to look steadily around.

And now it was for the first time that Lionel became aware of the fact that the Vampire was remaining comparatively still in the waters.

In a word, she was riding at anchor.

Once more Lionel looked around.

Instantly he recognised the place.

They were in the Bay of Dileloe.

The pirates were busily engaged in lowering and loading boats with empty casks for water and bales of goods for sale or exchange.

From the deck of the ship the island presented a very pleasant and inviting appearance.

In the distance rose up a perfect amphitheatre of hills, all thickly wooded.

There were pleasant valleys, fertile with every variety of vegetation; broad lakes and silver streams; while the brown woods were rendered delightful by the tall and stately palms, the fragrant citron, the odoriferous orange, and the grateful and delicious cocoanut.

Birds of beautiful plumage passed and repassed over head, filling the air with Nature's sweetest harmony.

Viewed from the deck of the schooner, the place seemed exactly what Captain Kydd had described it to be—

"Another Eden, demi-Paradise!"

Up on the shore were dragged a number of canoes and proas.

Several of these instantly put off for the ship.

They were manned by Africans of most war-like appearance.

Evidently the inhabitants of Dileloe were by no means to be despised.

Many signs of primitive civilisation were at once observable.

Captain Kydd seated himself in the prow of the gig.

Lionel and Hans Van Ryder were unceremoniously hustled into the same boat.

Nero was left in charge of the Vampire.

The longboat and the cutter alone accompanied the gig.

These were crowded with pirates all armed to the teeth.

All three boats were run ashore without the slightest difficulty.

The pirates were instantly surrounded by a number of Africans, many of whom were attired in picturesque costumes.

Captaid Kydd and his crew were evidently old acquaintances of the natives, who gave them the most friendly greeting.

"What, Captain Kydd!" exclaimed a gigantic

African, in very gaudy attire. "What," you come back again? King Bangalibaleo will be delighted to see you."

"I've no doubt whatever upon that score," returned the pirate, with that free-and-easy air so peculiarly his own. "I've brought him some splendid presents from the North. Englishmen are great engineers, and they are also especially noted for the manufacture of canister and grape, to say nothing of slugs and chain-shot. But how is trade, my buck?"

"Oh, the market's crowded," returned the African. "There are a lot of Arabian merchants, and a lot from Turkey, too, who are on the look-out for slaves."

"I don't do much in that line," replied Kydd. "But I've got a couple of whites to dispose of at a fancy price. Introduce a good customer, and I'll make you a present."

As he spoke Captain Kydd exhibited to the black a brace of pistols of antique manufacture.

The negro's eyes sparkled greedily.

"I will introduce to you lots of customers," he responded.

"Introduce to me one good one, and you shall have a powder-horn as well."

Captain Kydd knew the way to the market-place perfectly well, and although he knew that King Bangalibaleo had reason to regard him in an exceedingly hostile manner, he strolled onward beside the African with the air of a man who had long been in the habit of defying far mightier potentates than the King of Dileloe.

Lionel and Hans were seized suddenly by the pirates, who hurried them after their chief.

A very stout and important-looking Turk now advanced towards the pirate captain, and made a profound salaam.

"You are the owner of these slaves, I am told."

"I am," replied Captain Kydd. "From whence do you come?"

"I am a merchant, of Constantinople," the Turk replied, "and I am about to travel by land to Tripoli, whence I shall take ship and cross the Mediterranean. So, you see, if I purchase your slaves I shall have a great distance to travel and many dangers to encounter. Under the circumstances, what will you take for your slaves?"

Captain Kydd was a man of few words if he wished to drive a bargain.

His chief object in this case was to place our hero in perpetual bondage, from which there was no possible chance of escape, and under which he would have to suffer the greatest amount of hardship and punishment that a cruel and unrelenting master could impose.

"For what purpose do you employ your slaves?" he demanded.

"To work in mines," replied the Turk, "from which I never permit them to emerge. I allow them no wearing apparel; feed them on bread, rice, and water; set guards over them, who keep them at work, by means of the lash, for two-and twenty hours each day."

Captain Kydd broke out into an oath.

"By Jingo! you shall have the two for the

smallest piece of gold in your possession."

The Turk stared at him in astonishment for a moment, plunged his hand into his pouch, took a piece of gold at random, passed it to the pirate, and said—

"Give me a receipt."

Captain Kydd produced his pocket-book and hurriedly wrote the required memorandum.

The delighted Turk made another salaam, waved the receipt in the air, made a signal with his hand, and, pointing to Lionel-of-the-Sea and Hans Van Ryder, cried delightedly—

"They are mine. Chain them to the rest of the gang. We start to-night."

Two stalwart Nubians, with muskets slung across their backs, scimitars at their sides, and whips in their hands, advanced and rudely seized our hero and his friend.

The blacks marched our hero and Hans across the square to where a gang of thirty miserable natives were linked together with massive chains of iron.

Lionel-of-the-Sea knew it would be useless to offer any resistance.

Dark as the future seemed at that moment the star of hope yet glimmered and trembled before him.

Therefore, with as proud a bearing as he could assume, he suffered himself to be chained to his fellows in misfortune.

Kydd looked on with a sardonic grin of triumph.

The gang were chained so as to march two abreast.

CHAPTER XII.

THE DEPARTURE OF LIONEL AND HANS—KING BANGALIBALEO INVITES THE PIRATES TO A BANQUET, AND THE PRINCESS ZULU MAKES A VERY ASTONISHING PROPOSITION TO CAPTAIN KYDD.

OUR hero and Hans were placed side by side and their left wrists handcuffed together.

Their right arms were chained to the right arms of the two in front of them.

Thus all chance of escape was rendered impossible.

The merchant now mounted his camel, and all preparations were made to start.

The slave-drivers placed themselves on either side and behind the gang of unhappy captives.

Crack—crack—went their whips.

The long lashes darted and twisted about like snakes in all directions, and the yells and howls which ensued were something horrible to hear.

"Curse you," cried Lionel, aloud. "We shall meet again, Captain Kydd, and when we do, beware—Lionel-of-the-Sea will prove the conqueror yet!"

There was a rush of feet as the foremost of the slaves started into a run.

The others were obliged to follow at the same speed.

"Ha—ha!" laughed Captain Kydd, waving his hand mockingly. "A pleasant journey to you— farewell for ever."

Having thus disposed of our hero and Hans, Kydd went to the King's palace to dine with his majesty.

The king sat at the head.

Captain Kydd had a seat of honour on his right hand.

Then his majesty clapped his hands.

As he did so another curtain at the far end of the apartment was raised, and in came a number of women.

These were King Bangalibaleo's wives and daughters.

Amongst them, however, there was one girl much fairer than the rest.

And she was really and truly beautiful.

Her figure was perfect, her movements as full of grace as those of a gazelle, and as for her features there was very little of the African about them.

Her forehead was lofty, her nose delicately outlined, and her lips were chiselled, while her tresses, black and glossy as a raven's wing, hung in wavy masses around her neck and shoulders, instead of being short and curling closely to the head, like that of her companions.

"Who is she?" asked Kydd of the king.

"My daughter—the Princess Zulu," replied his majesty, with some show of pride.

"Ah! And how old is Zulu—I mean how many English years?"

"Sixteen," was the laconic reply, as his majesty took a spoonful of savoury soup.

"I thought so; but she is as fully developed as a young woman of five-and-twenty in our country," remarked Kydd. "I see she is a half-breed. Who was her mother?"

"A white woman," replied King Bangalibaleo. "A ship was wrecked, so we killed the men and I married the woman."

"Whew! Do you know the name of the ship?"

King Bangalibaleo nodded and dropped his spoon, plunged his hand into his breast, and drew forth a packet of papers.

These he handed to Captain Kydd.

Seizing them eagerly the pirate captain turned them over.

A smile flitted over his face as he drew one forth.

It was the list of the crew and passengers of the San Josef.

Of the latter there were only two.

Don Ricardo del Alamancia and Dona Lucia del Alamanza.

The pirate captain quietly folded up his papers and put them in his breast-pocket.

King Bangalibaleo stared at him aghast.

Scalding his mouth and throat until the tears sprang into his eyes, in his hurry to get rid of a spoonful of the steaming soup he had just raised to his lids, he stared at Captain Kydd in a manner which plainly indicated his intention to remonstrate.

"And what has become of the Spanish lady?" inquired Kydd, coolly.

"But the papers——"

"All right. How about the lady—is she alive

or dead ?"

"Dead—but—but——"

"How did she die ?"

"She trod on something," replied King Bangalibaleo, whose eyes rolled horribly in their——

"and fell ——"

"Fell where ?"

"On my—my dagger. Yes, that was it, she rod on something and fell on my dagger."

The pirate captain emitted a long, low whistle.

King Bangalibaleo made several attempts to get the papers from Captain Kydd without coming to an actual quarrel.

But they were all abortive.

The celebrated pirate created roars of laughter by the way in which he replied to the King of Dileloe's demands.

At last King Bangalibaleo gave up all further efforts to regain possession of the coveted documents.

He clearly saw that if he insisted it would cost him Captain Kydd's friendship and the loss of many lives.

And even then the pirate captain might prove the victor and still retain possession of the documents.

After all, too, King Bangalibaleo did not set any very great store by them.

So the feast went on, and the merriment was uninterrupted by any discord.

Some rum which Captain Kydd had sent for came in due course, and ere long King Bangalibaleo was sleeping comfortably with his arms and his head on the table.

The chiefs were no better than their monarch.

Indeed, the majority of them were so much worse that they were curled upon the floor in a state of blissful innocence as to their undignified positions.

But Captain Kydd and his men were much better able to withstand the effects of the powerful spirits.

Amongst the Europeans the grog circulated as freely as ever.

Consequently, the banquet-chamber was left to the undisputed possession of the whites and the women.

Captain Kydd lit his pipe and strolled to one of the windows which looked out into the gardens.

Here he stood.

But not long had he been there when, as he fully expected, the Princess Zulu came stealing up to his side.

Placing her hand on his arm, she looked straight into his eyes.

In an instant Captain Kydd read her character.

She was a woman in whose nature was mixed all that was tender and loving and all that was fierce and pitiless.

"What a woman for a pirate's bride," thought Kydd. "I must win her for myself."

And taking the small, soft, brown hand, he raised it to his lips.

She smiled, and inclined her head several times.

How elated Captain Kydd felt at that moment.

Fastly beat his heart with pride and joy.

Zulu's meaning was unmistakable ?

She loved him !

"My beautiful black pantheress," murmured the pirate, in a low and thrilling voice.

And he clasped her to his heart.

The Princess Zulu's face became radiant with delight.

Then she suddenly wrenched herself from the pirate's fervent arms, and throwing herself into a striking attitude, wonderfully full of command, she first pointed with her finger to her own breast, and then out through the open window towards the bay where the Vampire lay motionless on the still and glittering surface of the sea.

Captain Kydd comprehended her.

Then she uttered in broken English—

"Love ! Your wife !"

Very soft and thrilling was the tone ; very clear and precise the pronunciation of that word.

Then with rapid but exceedingly charming and graceful movements she pointed to her father, still sleeping, with his head on his arms, and the insensible chiefs wallowing on the floor.

She put on an expression of alarm.

She pointed through the window to the bay again, she clenched her fists, pressed her bent arms against her sides, and planting one foot firmly on the floor raised the other.

The attitude was that of a person running at full speed.

Zulu glanced meaningly at him, and nodded repeatedly.

"I understand," cried Captain Kydd.

A bird of beautiful plumage winged its way past the window.

Zulu pointed after it excitedly, and tapped her breast with the tip of her finger.

Captain Kydd, being a great swell in his own way, had his own Spanish page to attend him.

Beckoning this youth to his side he whispered some instructions to him, and young Pedro sped away down to the town to collect the men who were ashore and signal the Vampire to send another boat.

"Be quick all of you," said Pedro. "You know what the captain is when he gets excited."

The men knew well enough, so they went to work in as smart a manner as possible.

The boats were ready and the men seated at the oars when Kydd and Zulu appeared followed by a crowd of Africans, who seemed to be aware that he was running away with the king's daughter. Some threw spears, others shot arrows, and several of the boat crews were wounded.

Kydd himself received a scratch on the shoulder, and vowed to be revenged. But eventually all got safely on board the Vampire.

————◆◆◆————

CHAPTER XVI.

THE CAPTIVES—THE HALT—LIONEL-OF-THE-SEA ASTONISHES HANS VAN RYDER.

DREARY indeed was the prospect before brave Lionel-of-the-Sea and Hans Van Ryder.

Chains and slavery.

Slavery of the most cruel and awful kind—a bondage so full of horrors that the mere contemplation of such a doom is sufficient to turn the heart sick and make the blood run icy cold in the veins.

A living death in a dark mine—to toil unremittingly beneath the cutting lash, for rare jewels destined to deck the crowns of kings—to grace some lovely and happy being, or to flash and gleam on the neck and fingers of wantons, who spend their lives in reckless mirth and revelry.

Such was the fate to which they were being driven like a herd of wild cattle.

On with a rush trampled the slaves again.

Clank—clank—clank went the fetters, and mingled with the dismal rattling and jangling of the chains came the whistling and cracking of the slave-driver's whip.

The camels strode rapidly along.

But the poor iron-bound prisoners were compelled to keep pace with them.

On—on they ran, until the perspiration streamed from every pore—on until the strained sinews seemed ready to break asunder—on until red-hot irons seemed to be darting up and down in all their veins.

The sun's last burnished glow faded from the purple sky and the moon rose to shed her sweet pale light over the sad scene.

Serenely unmoved, the countless stars looked down upon the breaking hearts below.

By this time they had reached a large and open plain, bounded by a great forest on the west, and a rugged tract of land on the east, which led to the vast Kalahari Desert, which the merchant intended to cross.

The Kalahari Desert was about one hundred miles from the plain we have mentioned.

This open piece of ground the merchant deemed a suitable place for camping.

Therefore the slaves were ordered to halt again.

Never was command more willingly or more promptly obeyed.

The merchant descended from his camel.

His mounted attendants followed his example, and three tents were instantly pitched.

One of these was for the merchant's exclusive use.

The other two were for the occupation of his attendants.

Some coarse food and a small quantity of water served for the evening repast of the slaves, and their right hands were released from the fetters, that they might feed themselves.

Hans was very downhearted. Lionel seemed quite cheerful.

Our hero knew that he had concealed in his clothing a sharp file, which would easily cut through such soft iron as his fetters were made of, and he resolved as soon as it was dark to make the attempt.

Presently the three men who had been placed as guards lay down and went to sleep, and whispering his intention to Hans our hero set to work, the noise of the file being drowned by the chirping of some insects of the cricket tribe.

In a few minutes Lionel was at liberty, and then in an equally short space of time he set free his companion.

"We must arm ourselves," he whispered.

"How can we do that?"

Lionel pointed at the nearest sentinel, who was sleeping soundly with his sabre and gun by him. Creeping cautiously up to him Lionel stretched out his hand.

The tips of his fingers just touched the heavy iron mounting on the hilt of the sword.

His hand shook as he drew a few inches nearer and clasped it.

Hesitating not a moment, Lionel raised the weapon, and seizing the blade close to the point, pushed the hilt behind him.

Hans Van Ryder instantly clutched it.

Next he took the sleeper's long-barrelled gun.

This he likewise passed to his companion.

So far all had gone well.

The second sentinel was not more than a yard away.

Lionel-of-the-Sea wriggled his way towards him.

The man moved restlessly in his sleep.

Our hero crouched close to the ground.

Some muttered guttural words fell from the sleeper's lips.

Then all was still again.

The guard slept on.

Lionel drew a little nearer, and paused again for a moment.

With palpitating heart and starting eyes Hans Van Ryder watched his daring companion.

Lionel-of-the-Sea ventured still nearer to the restless slumberer.

Once again his hand clasped the hilt of a scimitar—a second later, and he grasped a musket also.

A feeling of unutterable relief came over him.

Noiselessly he glided back to his companion.

Then the two venturesome lads glanced round.

Everyone else was still wrapped in slumbrous repose.

"For a time we had better keep on the ground," whispered Lionel, "in case anyone should start suddenly up, or chance to turn his eyes this way. But be as rapid in your movements as possible."

Hans Van Ryder needed not this latter injunction.

He was exceedingly desirous of putting as great a distance as he could, in the shortest possible time, between himself and the camp of the Turkish merchant.

Lionel spoke not another word.

Slinging his gun across his back and placing the scimitar between his teeth, he made his way along at a speed which rather astonished his less active companion.

The young Dutchman, however, exerted himself

to the utmost and managed to keep pretty close to our hero, though the effort taxed him sorely.

For quite two hundred yards they proceeded in this fashion.

Then they came to a long line of thick bushes.

Once behind these and they would be effectually screened from the most searching observer.

Lionel sprang to his feet.

Nothing loth, Hans Van Ryder did the same.

The trees of the forest, which stood upon rising ground, were not more than three quarters of a mile distant now.

Once under the cover of that waving panoply of green, and their chances of escape would be increased a thousand-fold.

And now their hearts beat high with hope.

They had succeeded up to the present time far beyond their expectations.

Keeping well under cover of the bushes, both started into a run.

Fleet of foot as greyhounds were the two boys, and each now put forth his utmost powers.

After the first minute, however, Lionel distanced his companion.

He reached the forest a minute and a half before the young Dutchman

"You run splendidly," panted Hans Van Ryder, as he came tearing up. "Hitherto I have prided myself upon the fleetness of my feet, but you have beat me out of all time.

"Hush!" cried Lionel.

The faint but unmistakeable report of a musket struck upon their ears.

It came from the direction of the camp.

"Now," said Lionel-of-the-Sea, "clap on all sail, and we shall yet show them a clean pair of heels. Thank heaven we have a good start."

The two lads started forward at the top of their speed.

Lionel led the way.

It was by no means an easy one.

Heedless, however, of clothes and skin alike, they trampled over the thick undergrowth, and fought their way through seemingly impassable thickets.

But several times they heard shots.

But fainter and fainter each time seemed the reports.

Nevertheless, the excitement under which the two boys laboured was intense.

Their pursuers would naturally come to the conclusion that they had taken to the forest.

And as they had not the remotest notion of its extent, they could not, of course, feel certain that their enemies would not pounce upon them shortly in a most unexpected manner.

Keeping due west, they raced onward until sheer exhaustion compelled them to slacken speed, and ultimately to stop altogether.

They halted in a long valley between two high and thickly-wooded hills.

"I should think," panted Hans Van Ryder, "that we must be tolerably safe."

"If they find us," replied Lionel-of-the-Sea, "it can only be by the merest accident in the world."

"Just so. To look for two boys in a forest of such magnitude and dimensions, seems to me to be quite as hopeless as looking for the proverbial needle in the rick of hay."

"Exactly. What do you say to ascending this hill?"

And Lionel-of-the-Sea pointed to the more densely wooded of the two.

"By all means."

"It must command an extensive view of the surrounding country."

The two lads now commenced to ascend the hill.

This was a difficult task.

Not only was the side steep, but it required repeated efforts to surmount the many difficulties which met them at almost every step.

At length, however, their perseverance was rewarded.

They reached the top at last.

In consequence, however, of the thickness of the trees which crowned the summit, they could not see very far around them.

"One moment," cried Lionel.

And selecting one of the tallest trees, he climbed it with the agility of a monkey.

Ascending to the very topmost branch, Lionel-of-the-Sea shaded his eyes with one hand and glanced around.

Beams of pleasure made his young handsome face quite luminous.

There—far below, and opening out before him, was the wide ocean "girdled with the sky."

"Hurrah!" shouted Lionel, "Hurrah! The sea—the sea!"

Then suddenly remembering how far sounds travel in the still night-air, he stopped short and contented himself with waving his hand triumphantly.

The sight of the blue expanse was quite sufficient to fill with renewed energy and hope the heart and frame of Lionel-of-the-Sea.

He came down with as much celerity as he had run up the tree, and confronted Hans Van Ryder with flushed face and sparkling eyes.

"I have seen it," he cried.

"Seen what?"

"The sea—the glorious sea, Hans, over the foam-crested billows of which we shall yet ride in some stately vessel—the wide waste of waters upon the surface of which we shall yet meet Captain Kydd and his bloodthirsty horde! Hurrah! Hurrah! Yes, Hans—there it is, we shall encounter the pirate in his own element and have our revenge."

The two boy-heroes then looked about them for a place where they could rest with some degree of safety until the following morning.

They were not long in finding the much-required retreat. Quite close to the tree which Lionel-of-the-Sea had ascended, Hans Van Ryder discovered a small cave, the mouth of which was partly hidden by bushes.

Into this they crept.

A close examination satisfied them that no wild beast was crouching inside, and when Hans Van Ryder had lain himself on the floor in an attitude of repose, Lionel drew the bushes over the entrance in such a manner as to completely hide it from the view of their pursuers, should chance lead them that way.

To such hardy young adventurers, overcome with fatigue as they were, the hardest and roughest couch was as delightful, if not more so, than the softest bed of down to the enervated inhabitants of towns and cities, who have never known what real hardships are.

They were in a few minutes wrapped in the soundest slumber.

"Lionel! Lionel!"

Our hero knew that he was asleep and dreaming, yet he heard the voice as distinctly as if a bell had sounded close to his ear.

It was the voice of Vanderdeck

"Look, Lionel!" were the words of the vision.

Lionel-of-the-Sea seemed to stand upon the almost snow-white deck of a vessel.

Brisk sailors were climbing the taut rigging like cats, and running hither and thither in obedience to their superior officer's commands.

The sun was high in the heavens and the sea lay as smooth as a burnished mirror.

Not a breath of air stirred the sails, but a dark cloud just peeping above the western horizon told that a storm was coming.

Lionel looked about for Vanderdecken.

He had vanished, and none of the crew took the slightest notice of our hero.

"These are but the shadows of the past," a voice whispered in his ear. "Wait and see."

Lionel sat down and folded his arms.

All to him was as clear as day, and he could not convince himself that a spell was upon him, and what he gazed upon was a vision.

Presently he heard the loud sound of a voice from below.

Oaths, curses, and threats rent the air, as a handsome young officer, in a handsome uniform, ran up the ladder and sprang on deck.

The young man's face was pale, as if with terror, but his eyes flashed with an angry light.

"It is no use," he said, saluting another officer. "The captain will have his way, and not a sail is to be reefed. We are all dead men."

"Murdered men you mean," said the other. "In less than half an hour yonder storm will be upon us, and then——"

He ceased speaking, and lowered his eyes to the sea.

It had begun to heave and swell ominously, and a low droning sound announced the coming of the gale.

"Van Coots," said the officer who had spoken, "you have more power than I. Can you not reason with the captain? Most of the crew have loving wives and children waiting to greet them on shore. For myself I care nothing, for I have neither kith nor kin, but it would be a pity to send such brave fellows to the bottom of the sea."

Van Coots frowned and shook his head.

"I will do my best," he said, "though it costs me my life. You know the old saying, 'When wine is in, wit is out,' therefore I am certain that I shall only waste breath."

The last word had scarcely passed his lips when the captain of the vessel stepped on deck.

Lionel-of-the-Sea marked him well.

He was a tall, middle-aged man, of splendid proportions, which his rich uniform set off to great advantage.

Dark masses of hair flowed over his shoulders, and his eyes glowed like living coals.

"Unreef those sails," he cried, in a voice of thunder, "and set every stitch of canvas. I am master and owner of this vessel, and the man who does not wish to obey my orders may take service with Davey Jones by going overboard."

Lionel-of-the-Sea gazed at the speaker intently, and saw in his form and features Vanderdecken, as he had probably been in the prime of life.

"Captain," said Van Coots, "the elements under the hand of Providence are a million times stronger than your will. If you have no thought for yourself, think of others."

Vanderdecken drew his sword and thrust the point against Van Coot's breast.

"Give the order, or I will run you through," he cried. "I defy the power of Heaven, as I laugh at the powers of darkness. I will round the Cape in spite of all the winds that ever blew, in spite of all the lightning that ever tore clouds asunder, and in spite of all the seas that ever rolled mountains high. That is my oath, and if I do not keep it may I beat about these latitudes, or wander without rest between Hades and Heaven till the Day of Judgment."

With wonderful rapidity did Vanderdecken pour forth these utterances.

"Recal that awful vow," Van Coots almost shrieked. "Merciful Heaven be with us in this terrible hour!"

"Never!" Vanderdecken replied with a hollow laugh. "An oath once taken by me is never broken. Let storm, wind, and sea do their worst, I laugh, and mock at them all. When we land we will make merry, as we have always done. I am no child to be frightened by a capful of wind."

As he spoke the sky and sea turned black.

A huge wave, as if hurled upwards by some submarine eruption, arose, and curling over the stern of the vessel, struck it with a thunder-like crash.

Every timber creaked and groaned under the shock; but the mountain of water passed away, and then Lionel saw the men clinging in terror to whatever they could lay hands on.

Again came that mocking laugh from Vanderdecken.

He stood as firm as a rock, with his arms folded on his breast, his brows knitted, and his lips compressed into an ironical smile.

Suddenly a strange phenomenon appeared in the sky.

It was a terrific blaze of flame, but was not like lightning.

It had more the appearance of a giant's arm thrust from the flaming clouds; and then the vessel shivered from stem to stern under the stunning crash that followed.

"We are lost!" Van Coots cried, as he fell

upon his knees. "Mercy! Not to man I cry mercy, but——"

An immense volume of water swept over the vessel and drowned his utterance, and fearful shrieks rose above the din of the roaring waves and crashing thunder.

Though the storm had had no visible effect on Lionel-of-the-Sea, he started to his feet and ran to the spot where he had seen Vanderdecken standing.

He was no longer there; but presently another terrific blaze of lightning showed him lying against the bulwarks, where he had been driven stunned and senseless. Now the vessel heeled over, plunged, and wallowed helplessly in the trough of the sea.

The men had deserted the now useless pumps, and were gathered with the rest round the chief officer, who was throwing up his arms imploringly to the black raging masses covering the fair blue sky.

Though Vanderdecken could no longer resist the wishes of his men, it was too late to attempt to do anything, for the vessel had become a mere toy for the furious ocean to sport with.

It was flung hither and thither amid the foam, that flew like smoke, mast high; and Lionel, with his experience of seamanship, knew that the end could not be far away.

It came sooner than even he had expected.

Once more, with that terrible rush and roar, the mountains of waters swept over the parting timbers, and then all became a blank.

Lionel discovered that he had been borne gently to a rock, jutting out in mid-ocean, and presently he saw that Vanderdecken was at his side.

The storm had passed away, and all was still and calm.

"I thank you for this lesson," Lionel said. "You have shown me the great secret of your life."

"Yes, the cause of my downfall and wanderings," Vanderdecken replied. "Many years have passed away since that time. I have been bitterly punished for my sins, but rest will come at last. A voice, unlike any other voice I have ever heard, often tells me so.

"One word more," Lionel cried.

But the spectre had vanished; and Lionel slept.

CHAPTER XIX.

THE STRANGE VESSEL.

IT is time that we returned to Captain Kydd.

The notorious pirate having secured the princess put out at once to sea, laughing his pursuers to scorn.

"All goes well," Captain Kydd said, addressing Nero. "Fortune favours the brave, and I have taught those black rascals that I have shown no faint heart to win a fair lady."

The monster in human form laughed boisterously at his own joke, and the dusky lieutenant added his voice to the hideous mirth.

The cries of the enraged savages could be still heard, but the king's men had no chance of catching the Vampire, which danced over the rippling waves like a thing endowed with life.

The island of Dileloe died away in the distance until it became a mere streak upon the ocean, and Captain Kydd having made sure that all danger of pursuit was at an end, went down to the cabin where the Princess Lulu had been placed.

She greeted him with a smile and put out her daintily moulded hand.

"For such a woman I would face a thousand dangers and die a thousands deaths," Captain Kydd said, under his breath. "If this voyage ends well I will give up the sea and settle down quietly."

He was in the act of stooping to kiss the princess's hand when he was startled by a knock at the door.

"Confusion!" the pirate hissed. "Am I to have no peace. What now?"

"Your faithful Nero desires a word with you."

"Come in."

The lieutenant entered the cabin.

Captain Kydd saw in a moment that something had gone wrong, for a greenish pallor had settled on Nero's countenance.

"How now," said Kydd, "have you seen a ghost?"

"No captain," Nero replied, "a hundred thousand ghosts would not frighten me half so much. The very devil seems to be in the ship, for she will not answer the helm, and instead of sailing nor'-west by west, we are going due east, and *in the very eye of the wind.*"

"Bah! nonsense," Captain Kydd growled. "Don't talk such nonsense to me. Something must have gone wrong with the compass."

"Come on deck, and see for yourself," Nero said.

"I will return presently," Captain Kydd said, smiling as he waved his hand gracefully to the princess. "It seems to me that there is but one head with a brain in it on board this vessel, and if I were not here the Vampire would soon become a wreck."

Nero scowled and displayed his white gleaming teeth.

In sullen silence he followed Captain Kydd on deck.

The pirate chief examined the binnacle minutely, but could find nothing wrong there.

Then he took an observation of the sun, and discovered that the vessel was going entirely out of its intended course.

Cursing, raving, and tearing his hair, he paced the deck, and the men fell back from him in alarm.

They had been used to his paroxysms of rage, but they had never seen anything like this.

He foamed at the mouth and the veins on his brow stood out like whipcord.

"Well," he said, at last, "I care not where we go so long as we keep clear of Dileloe. Let the winds, the sea, and the Fates do their worst, I fear nothing."

"Beware!" said a voice close to his ear; "the shadow of doom is upon you, villain."

"Who spoke?" Captain Kydd cried, almost beside himself with rage and fright.

He glared furiously at Nero, but the black lieutenant only folded his arms and shook his head.

"You lie!" Captain Kydd almost shrieked, "you one and all conspire against my peace of mind."

"Your peace of mind," said the mysterious voice, "what peace of mind can a murderer and a pirate have?"

Captain Kydd grew almost delirious.

He drew his sword, and planting his feet firmly on the deck, stood like a tiger at bay.

"Show yourself, be you man or demon?" he cried.

At that moment Vanderdecken appeared.

Neither Nero nor the rest of the crew saw him.

Captain Kydd's eyeballs seemed to be seared at the sight of the ghostly figure.

His limbs refused their motion, and he could only stand and glare in horror at the spectre.

"See how he stalks," the pirate chief gasped, in thick accents. "Is there no man of all my crew who will rid me of him?"

"The captain is mad," the men whispered to each other.

Nero was of the same opinion, and advanced to pacify the terror-stricken pirate.

"Look!" Captain Kydd cried, as great beads of clammy perspiration stood out on his face; "he mocks me, his eyes shine like stars at night. Ugh! torture me not. Take my life, if you will, but haunt me no longer."

"Restore the princess to her father, release Lionel-of-the-Sea and Hans Van Ryder from slavery," Vanderdecken said.

"What more would you desire of me?" Captain Kydd demanded.

"Seclusion from the world and a life-long repentance," the spectre replied.

In spite of all the horror he felt the pirate chief replied with a mocking laugh.

"Now, by the heaven I offended, you are surely lost," Vanderdecken said.

He advanced, and placed his icy hand on Captain Kydd's brow, and in an instant his face grew so livid that it had the appearance of being almost luminous.

His arms fell helplessly to his side, his whole frame shuddered with a death-like tremour, and with a shriek that rang from stem to stern of the Vampire, he sank with a crash on the deck.

Nero looked down upon the pirate's prostrate form, and the light of triumph lit up his eyes.

"Until the captain recovers I am commander of this vessel," the black lieutenant said, in a voice of authority. "Bear him below, and see that he is well watched."

and the order was obeyed.

CHAPTER XX.
THE REVENGE.

THE lads did not awaken until the sun was high in the heavens.

Lionel-of-the-Sea was the first to awake.

Springing to his feet our hero pressed his hand to his bosom and gazed around him in a bewildered sort of way.

Then all at once there flooded back on his mind the recollection of the previous day.

"Rouse up—rouse up, Hans!" he cried.

And he shook his fellow-adventurer roughly by the shoulder.

Hans started to his feet.

"Hullo! What is it? Where am I?" he inquired. Then his memory also came back to him.

"What of them, Lionel?—the slaves I mean?"

Our hero laughed.

"I have heard nothing of them, and, as many hours must have elapsed since we escaped, I presume our enemies must have given up the pursuit as useless."

"Well," remarked Hans, "that rascally old merchant did not pay a heavy price for us; that's one thing."

"Therefore," retorted Lionel, "he will mourn our loss the more; for, although he paid much less for us than for any of the others, he could have obtained ten times the amount that they would fetch for either of us. Consequently, he has lost his best bargain."

"But then his agreement with Captain Kydd reduced us to the same value as the rest, for we were to be sent to work in the mines."

"Ha, ha, ha!" laughed Lionel-of-the-Sea. "Do you think the old rascal would have adhered to that part of the bargain? Oh, dear no!—certainly not! my dear Hans, while white slaves will fetch a fancy price anywhere."

"Particularly in the market at Constantinople."

"Just so. But come, Hans, we must be stirring."

And dashing the bushes on one side, our hero stepped out into the forest path.

Romantic in the extreme was the scenery which greeted him.

It had appeared beautiful in the moonlight on the preceding night, but it looked simply magnificent now in the glorious golden glare of the sun.

And the air was rife with nature's sweetest harmony.

There was something perfectly Edenic, not only in the loveliness of the foliage, but also in the songs without words, which were wafted from above on the perfumed air, as birds of rare and gorgeous plumage passed and repassed constantly above.

How strangely at variance with the horrors of the night before was this scene of beauty—were these sounds of rapture.

To our friends it seemed like the work of some kind enchantress.

"How beautiful!" cried Hans, appearing at the mouth of the cave.

"How magnificent!" exclaimed our hero.

"Never have I seen anything half so delightful."

"Oh yes you have, Hans Van Ryder. You have stood upon the deck of a graceful vessel; you have looked up at the white sails bellying out before the breeze, and then your eyes have wandered over the glittering miles of ocean—all rainbow hued, while your enraptured ears have been filled with the joyous screams of the wild sea-mews which have thrilled your soul with speechless bliss as they hovered and circled about in the sunbeams ! To the sea, to the sea !"

And in his enthusiastic love of the wide waste of waters below, in his impatience to reach the shore, he started forward at a run, and commenced the descent of a steep and precipitous path.

And yet it is perhaps scarcely remarkable that our hero should run to the sea and look to it for protection, as children when in trouble seek their mother.

In fine, the sea was his mother insomuch as he had been nurtured upon its broad and billowy breast.

Hans Van Ryder stood at the top of the path and looked over at our hero in mingled astonishment and horror.

Nor was the astonishment of Hans to be wondered at.

Glancing downwards from the summit of the hill, where the young Dutchman stood, it seemed little short of madness to attempt the descent.

A monkey or a cat would have hesitated before making the venture.

But with a step as sure and as swift as a chamois, our hero bounded downwards.

"Come on—come on, Hans !" he cried, ; "to the sea—to the sea !"

"I am coming," shouted Hans. "But not in your footsteps. I will join you on the beach."

And he started away at full speed.

Five minutes later and Lionel stood upon the beach.

He gazed out at the wide expanse of waters, heaving for miles before him.

But no sail could he see.

No white speck in the distance.

A hand was placed upon his shoulder.

Lionel-of-the-Sea started round.

A cry of amazement broke from his lips.

It was not, as he had expected, Hans Van Ryder.

No ! it was a very different figure indeed that stood at our hero's side.

Lionel-of-the-Sea uttered an exclamation of amazement, and started back. And no wonder.

The weird and spectral figure of Vanderdecken stood at his side.

"Behold !"

As his hollow voice sounded on the air, Vanderdecken raised his long shadowy arm and pointed over the white foam-crested waves.

Our hero followed the direction thus indicated with his eyes.

A flush of colour like the dawn of day spread over his cheeks and brow.

The pulsation of his heart quickened.

Far away was an object which gladdened his sight. A white speck gleaming in the distance.

A speck so small that scarcely any but the practised eye of a sailor would have discerned it.

And even to our hero it looked more like some white sea-wren hovering over the surface of the ocean than aught else.

But full well did Lionel-of-the-Sea know what that white speck really was.

"You see it !" cried Vanderdecken.

"Yes, yes," shouted Lionel-of-the-Sea ; and he clapped his hands. "I see it—I see it—a ship—a ship, and it is coming this way. Hurrah for the deep blue sea ! and hurrah for the white-winged ship ! Hans—Hans come and see what is here to be seen, and cry with me hurrah—hurrah !"

Almost mad with joy and excitement, our hero glanced round for his companion.

The young Dutchman, who had found another and less perilous way to the beach, now came round a corner of the cliffs and ran towards him.

"What is it ?" panted Hans.

"Don't be afraid, Hans," replied Lionel-of-the-Sea. "He is a friend, although he is a ghost."

"A ghost !"

Hans Van Ryder stared at our hero in blank amazement.

Once more Lionel turned towards the spectre.

With a cry of astonishment he staggered back, Vanderdecken was no longer there.

Like a wreath of smoke, he had melted away on the salt sea air.

Hans Van Ryder glanced all round him, and then stared at our hero in blank amazement.

A moment's silence succeeded.

"What do you mean, Lionel ?" he stammered. "Surely you have taken leave of your senses ! Surely your mind has given way under recent suffering and excitement ! What terrible hallucination is it that makes you rave like this ?"

"Rave—ha, ha ! I tell you I do not rave—it is no delusion, but a fact, Hans Van Ryder. Not one minute ago there stood here at my side, and on this shingle, the spectral form of Vanderdecken !"

"Then where is he now ?"

"He has vanished, he has gone as he came, without warning and in silence. But look out yonder, Hans—out there across the water, where I am pointing with my finger, and you will see the good ship that Vanderdecken showed to me, bounding and leaping through the waves to our rescue. See, nearer and nearer it comes like a racehorse to its goal !"

Hans Van Ryder shaded his eyes from the sun with his left hand and gazed in the direction our hero pointed out.

Then he, too, gave utterance to an exclamation of surprise and delight.

By this time, the white speck had so much increased in size, that it could now be fairly distinguished as a ship coming full sail towards them. The flush on our hero's face deepened.

"Now, confess, Hans Van Ryder," he said. "Was I not right when I cried 'to the sea—to the sea !' I knew it. I knew it—my heart yearns towards the ocean like a child's to its mother. On its broad and billowy heart alone, do I feel safe and happy ! There is something here, Hans," and he pressed one hand to his left breast, "which tells me that when my foes are in pursuit of me, and I am not strong enough to grapple with them, all I have to do is to run to the sea and stretch

LIONEL OF THE SEA.

out my arms and the sea will at once afford me refuge!"

CHAPTER XXI.

STRUGGLE WITH THE PIRATES—GREAT VICTORY.

As Lionel spoke, he extended his open hands towards the flashing brine, with such deep and unaffected enthusiasm, that the stolid and less romantic young Dutchman was filled with wonder.

Nevertheless he could not but feel that he himself was at that moment infused with similar sensations.

"If she does not alter her course," said Hans, who had never for an instant removed his eyes from the rapidly approaching vessel, "she will certainly sight us."

"Sight us, Hans—sight us! She will come straight to this very point and take us away.

"Lionel—Lionel, how excited you have become since we have been here! If you know the vessel as——"

"If I know the vessel! Ha! ha! I should know her among a fleet in a mist."

"Well, and what is her name?" demanded Hans, eagerly.

Our hero's reply was given with a perfect shout—

"The Revenge!"

Hans Van Ryder's eyes kindled with delight.

With redoubled interest he regarded the approaching vessel.

"Yes, Hans," continued our hero in the same enthusiastic manner, "it is his Britannic Majesty's frigate, the Revenge, and this is further proof that I did right in yielding to the impulse which urged me to make for the sea at once. Had there been a fairy on the beach here to greet us when we came, and to ask us which of all the ships afloat in the South Atlantic I should have preferred to come to our rescue, my reply would have been—The Revenge."

"Indeed!"

"Yes, Hans Van Ryder, for not only will she afford us safety, but she will also enable me to speedily fulfil my prophecy and to wreak my vengeance on that scourge of the ocean—Captain Kydd!"

With greater impatience than ever the two lads watched the progress of the vessel.

But great as was the speed made by the frigate, she seemed a long while approaching the shore.

The distance she had to cover was great, and the anxiety of the boys was great also.

Every five minutes seemed like an hour.

And how could they feel sure that at any moment the slavers would not make their appearance upon the scene.

It was an awful state of uncertainty to be in, and there is no torture greater than that of suspense.

Suddenly, as if it had sprang up from the depth of the ocean, another ship, almost as large as the Revenge, came in sight and poured a broadside into the British man-of-war.

Lionel was almost mad with excitement, but the phlegmatic young Dutchman stood quietly watching with deep interest the battle, which began in terrible earnest.

Scarcely had the boom of the stranger's guns died away when the Revenge replied to their audacity with shot and shell in such a manner as to cripple her.

Then the boats of the British ship were lowered, crowded with armed men, and rowed towards the assailant, while the two ships kept up a withering fire.

The pirates—for pirates they were—made a desperate attack to repel the British tars boarding her; but without effect. The brave sailors brought their muskets to bear upon the cut-throat crew, and fighting their way up the piratical bark they gained the deck.

After a desperate struggle the pirates were driven back with fearful slaughter, and the British tars, with a lusty cheer, proclaimed victory.

There was no mercy shown to the vanquished; they were fastened down below, and the crew of the Revenge returned to their boats.

They had scuttled the pirate barque, and they had scarcely regained the deck of their own gallant ship when the doomed craft lurched over and sunk to the bottom of the sea with its living freight.

A few minutes more and not a trace of the fearful battle was to be seen, and the Revenge came sailing on quietly towards the spot where our young friends stood in breathless amazement at the awful tragedy which had just been enacted.

With bated breath Lionel waited until the Revenge was within hailing distance.

Then pointing the muzzle of his musket to the sky, he pulled the trigger.

There was a flash and a bang.

Scarcely had its echoes died away when a puff of white smoke jetted out from the side of the frigate.

Boom!

The dull heavy sound of a cannon reverberated over the waves in reply.

The Revenge approached as near as she could with safety and a boat was lowered and rowed to the shore.

Lionel and Hans were at once taken on board the Revenge.

As our hero, with the agility of a monkey, clambered up the frigate's side and leaped on to the deck, a wild cry of delight greeted him.

Then a slender, fairy-like form rushed towards him, and a silvery voice cried out—

"Saved—saved!"

Lionel-of-the-Sea was lost in amazement.

Could he believe his own eyes and ears.

"Violet!" cried Hans Van Ryder, as he the next moment sprang over the bulwarks. "Violet Everleigh!"

Lionel-of-the-Sea clasped her to his heart.

The crew of the Revenge crowded round.

The young Dutchman staggered back as if from the blow of a sledge-hammer.

"Violet!" gasped our hero, in a whirl of amazement and delight. "Violet Everleigh! This seems incredible! Miraculous! How came you here?"

CHAPTER XXII.

CAPTAIN KYDD FINDS THAT HE HAS MADE A VALUABLE ACQUISITION, AND THE PRINCESS ZULU PROVES HERSELF WELL WORTHY HER POSITION AS THE PIRATE'S BRIDE.

IT was some hours before Captain Kydd recovered from the trance or torpor into which he had fallen. At length he came to himself, and a few goblets of wine and Zulu's caresses made him as amiable as he ever could be.

That same afternoon the look-out man gave notice of a sail in sight.

"She must be our prize, then," shouted Kydd, so prepare for action at once.

So far as could be made out at that distance the strange ship had the appearance of a homeward-bound trader from the Indies, and with the prospect of rich booty before them the pirates set to work with a will.

The guns were run out, and each man, armed to the teeth, was in his place.

"Is she near enough to give her a shot?" Nero asked.

"No!" Captain Kydd replied, as he picked up his glass, and took another survey. "She is sailing full broadside to us, and I cannot make out her name as yet." "Then," said the black lieutenant, "your eyes must have lent extra strength to the glass to be able to distinguish Lionel-of-the-Sea."

"True," the pirate replied, "I may have been mistaken, and yet I could have sworn that I saw him. Was it a vision?"

"Another of your fancies," Nero said, grimly. Captain Kydd turned fiercely upon him.

"If you mock me," he said with glittering eyes, "I will put you beyond the power of imagination. Shut your white teeth, and keep your ready tongue silent."

Nero backed a few paces, and clutched the jewelled handle of a dagger.

Quick as the movement was, and swift as the grasp was relinquished, it did not escape Captain Kydd's keen eyes.

"Yes," he said hoarsely, "I know what you would like to do, but don't try that on yet. The time has not come yet, if it ever will."

"I do not comprehend your meaning," Nero said, with a crestfallen expression of face. "You seem to have taken a sudden dislike to me, and in the hour of danger, when you require my services most, you go out of your way to insult me."

"Mere fancies," Captain Kydd returned, sneeringly. "Ha! yonder vessel is dying away in the distance. How comes that?"

Nero forgetting all his grievances in the excitement of the moment, rushed aft, and consulted the compass.

"By Hades!" he yelled, we are drifting back towards the island of Dileloe.

"You lie!" Captain Kydd cried.

His voice was more like that of a wild beast than words emanating from human lips.

In an instant he was at the black lieutenant's side, and seeing at a glance the truth of his observation, he rushed below to consult his charts.

Then Captain Kydd fell into another paroxysm of rage, and blind to the presence of the lovely Princess Zulu, who had been brought safely on board, and deaf to her soothing words, he stamped and raved until his face grew purple, and truly awful to behold.

"If the Vampire strikes upon the hidden rocks surrounding Dileloe," he cried, in a furious, yet despairing voice, "we are lost. This accursed vessel seems to be endowed with a will of its own."

"Not so," said a sepulchral voice in his ear. "It is the will of heaven."

As the expression of Captain Kydd's countenance changed to one of death-like pallor, the Princess Zulu stared at him in blank astonishment.

"What ails you?" she asked. "Did I not know you so well, I should think that you had taken leave of your senses."

"It is nothing," the pirate said, brushing his hand across his clammy brow. "I thought I heard a strange voice, but it may be that my nerves are unstrung."

The Princess Zulu drew shudderingly to his side.

"I feel as if there were some strange and awful presence near," she said. "What is it? Tell me. Something falls upon me like a pall. Oh, protect me. I faint, I die."

As she swooned, he caught her in his strong arms, and at the same moment a hollow mocking laugh rang through the cabin."

"Fiend!" Captain Kydd shrieked, "Do your worst. I will be even with you yet. You are powerless to harm me."

"Beware!" said the well-known voice of Vanderdecken, "Your time on earth grows short. Look deep into your bad black heart, and turn from its evil promptings."

Half mad, Captain Kydd answered with an oath, and placing the princess on a couch, he rushed on deck again.

The vessel espied in the distance was no longer to be seen. "That fool at the masthead must have mistaken a seabird for a ship," Kydd growled.

Onward, over the bright blue waters, bounded the pirate schooner, and soon did the land fade from the sight, even of the man at the masthead.

Zulu stood upon the quarter-deck, gazing around with mingled wonder and delight.

There was something in the scene that was congenial with her warm impulsive nature.

A thrill of rapture ran through the pirate's veins as he watched her, and his eyes sparkled like diamonds.

No longer did he think of Violet Eversleigh.

To the fierce ocean ranger, what comparison did the pale and timid maiden bear to this strange and lovely creature who had so voluntarily surrendered herself to him?

None whatever.

The more he looked at Zulu the more enamoured of her he became.

Twenty-four hours passed. Kydd was in his cabin with Zulu.

Tap—tap—tap.

Someone was knocking at the door.

"Come in."

The door opened, and the gigantic form of Nero appeared at the entrance.

"Well, Nero, what is it?"

"A sail," replied the sable lieutenant. "But he's so far ahead that we cannot make her out at present."

"Humph! Can you form no opinion of her?"

"None whatever. I've had the glass upon her for the last few minutes, but all I can make out is that she is a three-masted vessel of some kind."

"Do you think it is the Revenge?"

The black lieutenant gravely shook his head.

"I scarcely think so—yet, nevertheless, it is quite possible. You see you can never tell when and where that accursed cruiser is likely to turn up."

"Truly. Well I'll be on deck in a minute or so, and by that time we shall be able to get a better view of her."

Nero bowed himself out of the cabin, closed the door, and stepped on to the deck.

"Now," cried Captain Kydd, turning once more to Zulu, "since you can use this sword you shall carry it. When next you appear on the deck it shall be as a pirate's bride ought to be seen."

Throwing open one of the ottomans, Kydd turned over a quantity of fine Indian clothing.

Selecting a turban, he placed it round Zulu's brows in the form of a turban.

With a shawl he wreathed her waist.

In this he placed a brace of pistols, the long shining barrels of which were beautifully inlaid with curious veins of gold, while the butts were mounted heavily with the same precious metal, and also a long curved dagger in a richly-chased and golden sheath.

Then to her side he buckled the scimitar she had so greatly admired.

Laughing pleasantly, he seized Zulu by the shoulder, and turned her round to the glass once more.

An exclamation of delight escaped her, and stamping her foot upon the floor, she shook her turbaned head with an air of defiance.

"Bravo!" cried Captain Kydd, as he clapped her on the shoulder. "Hurrah for the pirate's bride! And now to the deck once more."

Turning on his heel, he threw open the door.

With a stately air she marched out and glanced proudly around.

She was greeted with a thunderous cheer.

"Hurrah for the pirate's bride!"

The crew went nearly wild with excitement and admiration, for at once they recognised in the Princess Zulu a fitting mate for their daring and lawless leader.

Captain Kydd also received an enthusiastic salutation.

Over the salt-sea waves rang the lusty cheer of the pirates.

Stern, determined, and ruthless as he was, Captain Kydd was indeed a hero in the eyes of his fierce crew.

The beau-ideal of a pirate chief.

And Zulu promised to be equally popular.

Her lovely face, her faultless form, her bold haughty air of defiance, and free, graceful, and elastic step, all combined to win from that savage and motley crew admiration and respect.

Again and again the cheers resounded through the ship, and went echoing over the pleasant waters of the South Atlantic.

Captain Kydd waved his cap in acknowledgment as he stepped on to the quarter-deck.

Here stood Nero gazing intently through his glass at the distant ship.

"Well, do you make her out yet?" inquired Kydd.

"She certainly is not the Revenge," replied the negro.

Captain Kydd brought his glass to bear upon the far ship likewise.

The Princess Zulu kept close to his side.

There was a brief silence.

It broke suddenly.

"A prize! A prize!" cried Captain Kydd; "shake out every rag of canvas to the breeze, and clear the deck for action—we shall have to fight, for she is a large Spanish merchantman, and well armed."

This information was received with a cheer.

Up aloft into the rigging sprang the eager pirates.

With a smartness that would have done credit to the British navy the pirates handled their craft.

Every sail seemed set as if by magic.

Under a perfect cloud of canvas the Vampire coursed through the waves, with her masts bending like reeds, and her prow dashing the salt white spray before, like snow-flakes in a driving wind.

Zulu clasped the pirate's left hand in her own, and her eyes seemed to lighten as they roamed over the hissing brine.

The distance between the two ships decreased rapidly.

Like an eagle on the wing the Vampire swooped towards her prey.

At present those on board the armed merchantman were unable to form the slightest notion in regard to the character of the schooner.

An hour of anxiety and excitement flew past.

At the expiration of this time the Vampire had gained so much upon the merchantman that the two ships could now make out distinctly what was going on on each other's decks.

Just before, however, they came within hailing distance, the practised eye of the pirate chief detected signs of uneasiness on board the Spaniard.

Captain Kydd sprang upon a gun, and waving his sword shouted—

"Prepare for action. Run out the guns, and send a broadside into her."

The Princess Zulu would have followed him,

but he cried hoarsely to the crew to hold her back, and two men seized her with gentle firmness by the wrists.

"You may hold me now," she said, in her own language, "but when the fight is at its height I will shake myself free, and join in the fray."

The villanous crew, with bloodthirsty eagerness, obeyed the order of Captain Kydd, and a volley of shot and shell was showered into the luckless Spanish bark.

The shots took effect, the ship was seen to reel over as the shower of iron missiles struck her, and the Spaniards were thrown into a state of fearful consternation.

There was a sudden commotion on the deck of the merchantman.

The sailors ran hastily to and fro.

Then the yards swung round and her helm was put to starboard.

Thus the direction of the vessel was altered.

"Hard-a-port!" cried Captain Kydd.

The command was instantly obeyed.

Magnificently the schooner answered to her helm, and the next minute the Vampire was cutting through the water with unabated speed, and in such a direction that unless the Spaniard again altered her course, she would in the course of another half-hour, get right athwart her bows.

This movement on the part of the schooner failed not to have a very natural effect upon the captain of the merchantman.

It naturally increased his alarm.

More canvas was clapped on.

At a greatly increased speed did the Spaniard tear through the water.

But vainly did her masts bend, her cords creak, and timbers groan.

With white and outspread wings the Vampire sped towards her.

Minute by minute the distance was visibly decreased.

No amount of tacking on the part of the Spaniard could baffle the pirate.

Captain Kydd was a consummate sailor, and the Vampire was unquestionably the lightest-heeled craft afloat.

It soon became evident to the Spaniard that all chance of escape by flight was at an end.

Excepting surrender, he had but one alternative.

That was to fight.

By this time Captain Kydd was able to make out the name of the frigate.

The San Josef.

That was the name printed in gold characters along the stern gallery of the Spanish merchantman.

The pirate no sooner made out this name than he produced a list from his breast-pocket, down which he ran his finger for some distance.

Captain Kydd started to his feet.

"Up with our flag," he cried, "let our dreaded ensign flutter from the masthead. Run out the guns, and throw off all disguise. Ahoy, ahoy! It is the San Josef, homeward bound from Cape Town with a cargo of gold!"

* * * * * *

Violet Eversleigh did not reply immediately to our hero's question.

She was too much overcome with astonishment and delight to give any account of herself just then.

A number of blue-jackets crowded round the two young adventurers and the lovely girl.

Captain Canon and several officers now approached.

The former was a fine, handsome, dashing-looking fellow, just in the very prime of life, and there was something particularly engaging alike in his smile and manner of address.

He was a great favourite with the crew.

And he deserved to be, for there was not in the whole British Navy a more able and gallant commander than Captain Canon.

"Hullo!" he cried, "what means this! An unexpected recognition, eh?"

"Miss Eversleigh," explained Hans Van Ryder, "was a passenger on board my father's ship, The Queen of the Zuyder Zee, which was attacked by Captain Kydd."

"Ha, ha! Miss Eversleigh told me about that; you are the son of Captain Jan Van Ryder, who was murdered!"

"I am."

"Give me your hand, Hans," cried the Captain. "From Miss Eversleigh's lips I heard the account of your brave deferce of her. By Jove, you are a splendid fellow. And who is this?"

Captain Canon waved his hand towards our hero.

"I will speak for myself—I am Lionel-of-the-Sea."

And our hero, with Violet clinging to his side, turned to face Captain Canon.

The commander of the Revenge regarded him critically.

The twinkle of his blue, fearless eyes, indicated that he was perfectly satisfied with the result of his scrutiny.

"Lionel-of-the-Sea!" he echoed; "what a curious name! How came you by it? Have you no other name?"

CHAPTER XXIII.

ON BOARD THE REVENGE.

"I HAVE no other name," said Lionel-of-the-Sea, "and in reply to your first question I must tell you that it was given to me by no less celebrated a personage than Captain Kydd!"

"Captain Kydd!"

Captain Canon's visage assumed an expression of utter surprise.

"Even so," continued our hero. "I am an ocean waif—that is, if the pirate speaks the truth, about which I have my doubts sometimes—and was picked up by the crew of the Vampire after a fearful storm, during which many vessels perished.

"And you have been with the pirate ever since."

"Most certainly," answered Lionel. "He reared me as if I had been his own son, and if you an believe that a man of Captain Kydd's ferocious nature is capable of any affection for a living creature—he is—or was, strongly attached to me."

"I do believe that such a thing is possible," remarked Captain Canon; "for I am inclined to think that the worst of men have some traits in them that are wholly at variance with their general characters. However, be that as it may—I will see you in my cabin after you have replied to one or two questions."

Lionel-of-the-Sea bowed his head in assent.

"In the first place then—did you, while with Captain Kydd, serve under him?"

"In what way?" asked our hero. "If you ask me whether I used to fight under his accursed flag—if I used to take part in the dreadful scenes of blood, rapine, and murder, I am prepared to swear before my Maker that I have never upon one single occasion done so! No! Many and many a time has Captain Kydd endeavoured to force me by threats and blows to join his men in their fiendish work; but although brought up amidst such outrages, and accustomed as I have been from my earliest infancy to such terrible spectacles there was something here," and he pressed his hand to his heart, "which forbade me to join my companions in their hellish exploits, the mere thought of which was most revolting to my nature."

To have doubted our hero when he made this declaration would have been almost impossible.

With such fervency, in fact, did he give utterance to the words that his cheeks flushed and his eyes flashed as he raised his disengaged hand as if calling Heaven to bear witness to his truth.

"Good," cried Captain Canon. "That is sufficient. I believe you most completely, for I have looked closely into your face, and I pride myself upon being able to read anyone's character there correctly. I shall, therefore, reserve other questions I mean to put to you until we are together in my cabin."

"Thank you, sir,"

"And as for you, Mynheer Van Ryder, I wish to see you immediately—please step this way."

And Captain Canon strode towards his cabin.

Our hero, with Violet at his side, walked to the quarter-deck, and, after replying to such questions as the officers put to him, signified his desire to be left alone with his fair companion for a while.

The midshipmen were by no means easily shaken off.

Indeed, had it not been for Lieutenant Webber, our hero would have been pestered to death by those inquisitive and mischief-loving young monkeys.

At last, however, our hero and heroine found themselves comparatively free.

Lionel perched himself upon a carronade.

Violet leaned against the taffrail and upturned her lustrous eyes to his.

"This is a strange reunion," remarked our hero.

"And a happy one——"

"Yes, a happy one, Violet—I may call you Violet, may I not?"

"Most certainly. I think when people have been thrown together in so singular a way as we

have been, that they ought not only to drop all formalities, but also to regard each other in much the same manner as they do their blood relations."

"And so do I," coincided Lionel, with much warmth, "but to return to our original topic—you know I am still in ignorance as to the manner in which you came to be aboard this ship."

Violet's face flushed.

"You have not forgotten our parting?"

"Oh, no."

Violet shuddered.

"I thought when the pirate seized me in his arms and carried me away that all was over—that all three would perish—for I had made up my mind to die rather than to submit."

"Yes, yes."

"Well, he put me in his cabin, but before he had time even to speak to me he had to return to the deck."

"I know it—and the reason also—there was a phantom ship."

"Yes. Well, Captain Kydd, when he left me, locked the cabin door, and I was on an ottoman in a half-fainting condition.

"Rapidly and painfully was my heart beating at that moment.

"I made sure that both you and Hans would be butchered forthwith, and that, unless I made away with myself at once, a fate still more horrible awaited me.

"I waited several moments, and then, starting up, looked about.

"Weapons of all kinds were hung around, and on the table was a naked sword and a brace of pistols.

"I instantly seized one of the latter.

"At least I had the means of preserving my honour, and, knowing full well that the miscreant would not give me a moment's grace on his return, I uttered a prayer for pardon, and prepared to blow out my brains forthwith. Do you blame me?"

"Blame you, Violet! No, on my soul, I do not. I respect—I honour you the more for making such a resolution."

Violet's face brightened with pleasure.

"'Oh, heaven help me, was my prayer,' as I pointed the pistol at my head.

"My finger was on the trigger, and I should have pulled it in another second, only I was interrupted in a manner so strange and startling that I nearly swooned.

"'Hold!' sounded a strange voice; 'Hold, rash girl.'

"I started and looked round, and behold, standing at my side was a tall, stately, spectral figure.

"'Fear not!' he cried, 'Fear not, Violet Eversleigh—I am here to save you.'

"Welcome as this announcement was, I must confess my blood froze in my veins at beholding this apparition.

"Nevertheless, I regarded him attentively, and saw he was attired in Vandyke costume, and furthermore that his garments were saturated with

B

water which dripped from him in such quantities that quite a pool had already collected at his feet."

"Ah!" exclaimed our hero, "it was the Phantom Vanderdecken, whose ship was at that very moment flying past the Vampire."

"It was, as I immediately afterwards discovered, for without any further ceremony he clasped me in his arms, and together we sank through the floor of the cabin.

"I shrieked with terror.

"'Fear not,' he cried again. 'I am Vanderdecken.'

"After that, I remember no more.

"There was a rush of water over my head, and then—oblivion.

"When I recovered from my trance, which must have lasted some hours, I discovered myself lying on a couch, in what I afterwards found to be the state cabin of this frigate.

"My clothes were all dripping with water.

"Amazed, bewildered, and half-fearful that I was still on board the pirate ship, and had only been dreaming, I started to my feet.

"As I did so, the door of the cabin was thrown open, and Captain Canon entered.

"That was the first time I had ever seen him.

"Therefore you may imagine how great was his astonishment at finding me in his cabin, and in such a condition.

"It was some time before I could induce him to believe my story, which certainly is one of the wildest, strangest, and most improbable that can be conceived."

"Nevertheless it is true."

"Perfectly. But see—Captain Canon is approaching."

Lionel-of-the-Sea raised his eyes from those of Violet Eversleigh's, and saw Captain Canon step on to the quarter-deck.

Our hero at once sprang off the carronade.

CHAPTER XXIV.

THE FATE OF THE SAN JOSEF.

"A-H-O-Y—A-hoy! It is the San Josef, homeward bound from Cape Town, with a cargo of gold!"

"Hurrah!"

A fierce wild cheer resounded on the air as the pirates, emerging from their place of concealment, bounded to the centre of the deck or rushed to the bulwarks.

A more ferocious-looking set of bloodthirsty miscreants could not possibly be imagined, as with cutlasses flashing in their hands, dirks held in their teeth, and pistols and muskets clutched convulsively, they dashed hither and thither.

All disguise, of course, was thrown off the moment the black flag, with its curious device, fluttered from the masthead.

Captain Kydd raised a speaking trumpet to his lips.

"A-hoy—a-hoy—a-hoy!"

That lusty hail might have been heard at three times the distance there was now between the two ships.

No notice, however, was taken of it.

The captain of the San Josef was afraid to cl on any more canvas, as the strain was already t great upon the masts, which threatened, as it w to give way under the fearful pressure.

But, with every rag spread to the freshenir breeze, the saucy pirate schooner ploughed throug the water, at a rate which filled with amazeme the crew of the Spanish merchantman.

In fact, in comparison with the Vampire, t San Josef was but a lubberly craft after all.

Nearer and nearer came the two vessels togethe

The rate at which the Vampire was gaining the San Josef was truly astonishing.

Every minute decreased the space between h and the San Josef palpably.

"San Josef, a-hoy!" cried Captain Kydd agai "haul up, lay to, or curse me I'll sink you."

"Who are you?" demanded a voice from th Spanish vessel.

"Captain Kydd, and this ship is the Vampire, replied the pirate. "Am I to fire?"

A puff of white smoke jutted from the bows the San Josef.

Boom!

A ball splashed into the water, just beyond th stern of the schooner.

"Whew!" whistled Captain Kydd, "she mea mischief. Now then Nero, let her have it."

The black lieutenant had been superintendin the working of a long brass cannon, upon whic the pirates set much store.

As Captain Kydd spoke, the link was applie to the touch-hole.

There was a flash, and a stunning report.

Eagerly the pirates watched for the result of th shot.

With a crash that was audible on board th Vampire, the foremast of the San Josef went b the board.

A cheer greeted the accomplishment of thi feat.

The shot, however, was replied to right bravel by the Spanish merchantman.

A whole broadside was directed against th Vampire.

The guns, however, were not so well served a they should have been.

Another broadside from the Vampire silence her guns effectually.

"Haul down that gaudy rag!" roared Captai Kydd. "The black flag alone waves triumphan over the waters of the South Atlantic. Give he another dose of pills."

Once more from the Vampire's sides came re flashes and white puffs of smoke.

The crashes and yells that followed were trul terrific, and when the smoke cleared away th San Josef lay like a log of wood in the water.

She was quite crippled.

Captain Kydd issued some orders in regard t the handling of the schooner, which, in a fe minutes more, was actually alongside the illfate craft.

Then down from the rigging and over th bulwarks leapt and sprang the pirates, all armed to the teeth and ready to commit any act o atrocity.

"Repel boarders," yelled the Spanish captain.

And then a most terrific hand-to-hand encounter ensued.

"Hurrah!" cried Captain Kydd, "Hurrah!" come on, lads. No quarter—gold!—gold!—gold!"

With frantic and fiendish yells the pirates, one and all, set up that fearful chorus.

"No quarter—gold!—gold!—gold!"

High over the clash of steel, the rattle of musketry, and the frequent report of the pistols, rose that dreadful cry for the accursed metal to possess which men will go to any extreme——

"Gold, gold, gold!"

Sabres clashed, firearms sent their deadly leaden messengers in all directions. Shrieks, cries, groans, and shouts of exultation, all commingled made a hideous and groaning chorus.

The deck grew red and slippery with blood.

And the mere sight of those crimson streams seemed to render the pirates more ferocious than ever.

Nero strode from stem to stern of the vessel, and then back again, dealing death with every blow of his broad and terrible scimitar.

Indeed, so conspicuous did the gigantic and picturesquely attired negro make himself that he might easily have been mistaken for the leader of the pirate horde.

But though Captain Kydd did not seem so full of bustle and excitement, it was seen and felt that wherever he went his fighting capabilities were far in excess of those of any one engaged.

In his cool and deliberate business-like way, Captain Kydd was extremely busy.

Without any evident exertions he sent the Spaniards reeling this way and that, or made them measure their length upon the deck never to rise again.

Everyone else seemed covered in blood, and smoking with heat.

The Spaniards fought desperately too, and for a length of time they kept the murderous crew back, until they were outnumbered and Captain Kydd's crew poured over the vessel's sides.

The Spaniards had only to fight and to die.

The cry of "quarter" was invariably responded to with a laugh of derision and the stroke of a sabre.

"Ah! you at least shall not live to revel with the spoils of the San Josef. Monster, take that."

And the Spanish captain aimed a blow at the bare head of the pirate chief.

The pirate laughed as he parried the stroke.

Then the two captains went to work with terrible earnestness.

Nero was in his element.

The gigantic negro strode about the deck, dealing death at every stroke with his flashing blade.

But there was another besides Captain Kydd and his terrible lieutenant, who seemed to be dreaded quite as much by the crew of the San Josef.

This was no other than that remarkable girl—the beautiful princess Zulu.

With a spring like that of some sleek pantheress she bounded on the deck of the Spanish merchantman, with a pistol in one hand and her splendid scimitar in the other.

Her appearance on the scene produced a most startling effect.

The Spaniards recoiled whichever way she turned.

Nor is this to be wondered at.

With her long, black silken hair waving and fluttering to the breeze, like the dread ensign that fluttered above; her eyes blazing, her nostrils distended, her beautiful lip curling, and showing her wonderfully white and tightly-clenched teeth, she appeared in very truth a lovely but dreadful demon.

Lithe were the movements of her supple limbs, and her springs were as sudden and as deadly as those of a tiger.

A tall Spaniard, who had knocked down several of the pirates with a heavy handspike, had crept behind Captain Kydd.

The weapon was already raised for the fatal blow, and Captain Kydd was quite unconscious of his peril.

Indeed, but for the quick eyes, and equally rapid movements of the dark Amazon, his career would have terminated on the spot.

But Captain Kydd's time had not yet arrived.

With a fierce cry, Zulu sprang upon the man.

There was a flash as of lightning, and the Spaniard went reeling to the deck, with a fearful gash across his breast.

Wildly her laugh rang out as she sprang into the thickest of the fight.

Kydd made a skilful feint, and passed his sword through the Spanish captain's breast.

"Hurrah!" he cried, springing to Zulu's side and striking down all who came within the sweep of his terrible blade. "Hurrah for the Black Flag! Ho! ho! Vampires, behold your queen, and imitate her example. Down with every Spanish drone! We fight for gold, boys! Gold! Gold! Gold!"

"Gold! Gold!"

The cry was taken up by the pirates; who, one and all, shouted it forth at the top of their voices, and there was a fierce and fearful ring about the word, which made the Spaniards shudder.

"Gold! Gold!"

Fainter and feebler each moment became the resistance of the Spaniards, who, however, fought to the last of their blood and their breath.

Indeed they knew full well that no mercy would be shown them by their pitiless foes, even if they had given over the hopeless fight and flung down their swords.

Frequently the dreadful shout rose high above the hideous tumult of the strife—

"No quarter—no quarter! Death to all! Gold—gold—gold!"

That was the word that seemed to drive the pirates to still more frantic exertions, and to excite them to commit still greater atrocities.

But lower and lower became the clang and clash of steel on steel—less and less frequent the sharp

and sudden reports of the pistols, or the ping—!
ping—! ping ! of the bullets.

At last the crew of the San Josef was reduced
to five.

And of these three were already wounded.

They stood in a knot at the gangway.

There was a look of calm and resolute despair
upon their countenances as they looked round
upon the crew of yelling and bloodthirsty miscreants.

"No quarter—gold—gold—gold !"

There was a rush from all parts of the ship.

A clash of steel.

Groans and shrieks.

Yells of delight and triumph.

There was a sudden hush.

All was over.

The last defender of the San Josef had been
stricken down.

"Hurrah !" cried Captain Kydd, waving his
flashing blade with triumph in the air. "Hurrah !
The gold is ours !"

The pirates yelled with delight.

"The gold is won !" cried Captain Kydd, "and
now lads to work. Get every ingot and stiver on
board the Vampire and then we'll send the San
Josef to the bottom of the sea, so that no one will
ever know what became of her."

"Hurrah !"

The pirates dispersed.

A number of them quickly disappeared below,
and immediately afterwards the precious cargo
was unceremoniously bundled on to the deck.

But while this animated scene was being enacted
a hail came from the Vampire which caused all to
start.

"Sail, ho !"

Captain Kydd uttered a cry, and sprang on to a
large bale of merchandise.

"Where away ?" he demanded, with his hand
to his mouth.

"On the larboard bow !"

Captain Kydd shaded his eyes with his hands,
and looked in the direction indicated.

There was no need for straining of eyesight.

In full view, and with stud-sails set, was a
magnificent frigate, bearing rapidly down upon
them.

During the fearfully exciting scene which we
have described, her approach had not been noticed
by the pirates until she was almost within gun-
shot of them.

Captain Kydd uttered a shout.

Signs of consternation and terror were instantly
observable amongst the pirates, who, one and all,
paused in their work.

"The Revenge !" shouted Captain Kydd, in a
voice that electrified all. "Death and fury ! In
five minutes more she will be within gun-shot,
and we have not yet an ounce of the gold for which
we fought on board the Vampire."

CHAPTER XXVI.

CAPTAIN CANON MAKES SOME INQUIRIES OF
LIONEL-OF-THE-SEA—THE VAMPIRE IN SIGHT.

"WILL you step with me into my cabin, Master
Lionel ? I have some queries to put to you."

"With pleasure."

Lionel made a very low bow.

He was fully sensible of the fact that in coming
instead of sending for him, Captain Canon paid
him a very high compliment.

He followed the commander down the steps to
the state cabin.

It was very handsomely furnished.

Captain Canon sat down at the table, on which
were scattered charts, maps, papers, and some very
fine Venetian glasses.

"Take a chair, Master Lionel."

Our hero did so.

Captain Canon filled a couple of glasses with
some light amber wine, and pushed one of them
towards Lionel.

"Your health, Captain Canon."

The commander of the Revenge bowed and drank
a little of the wine.

"I presume," he said, "that as you have been
with this celebrated pirate since your infancy, you
know all about his affairs ?"

"Unquestionably I know a great deal concerning
them."

"Ah ! That is just it. Now, I think you will
be able to render me most material service. Now,
where does the pirate stow his treasures ?"

"On an island."

"An unknown one ?"

"Oh yes ; it is a very out-of-the-way place on
the western coast of Africa."

"Do you know its latitude and longitude ?"

"Quite well—10 deg. W. long., 30. S. lat."

Captain Canon noted it down in his log.

"Very good. Now what do you say to the
practicability of taking possession of the island
and waiting there for the pirate to return.

Lionel-of-the-Sea shook his head.

"What are your objections ?"

"In the first place, Captain Canon, the island
is so strongly fortified and garrisoned, that it
would be the work of months for you to take it.
Besides, the batteries are so formidable that the
pirates might even succeed in sinking the
Revenge."

"Hum."

Captain Canon thoughtfully stroked his beard.

"Well, I shall certainly attack the island," he

"Sail ho !" sang out a voice from the masthead.

In an instant all was excitement on board the
Revenge.

Captain Canon at once made his appearance
upon the deck.

At present all that could be seen, even by the
aid of a powerful glass, was a speck of white in
the distance.

Everyone was on the tip-toe of expectation.

Captain Canon and several officers at once took

their stand on the quarter-deck.

"Now, Master Lionel-of-the-Sea," cried Captain Canon, "what do you think—will she or will she not turn out to be the pirate?"

"I think the odds are very greatly in favour of that distant ship turning out to be the Vampire," replied our hero, "for she is just in the very place where I should have looked for her."

This reply created quite a sensation.

With wonderful rapidity our hero's answer circulated throughout the frigate, and the eager tars crowded to the bulwarks, or swarmed up the rigging where they could obtain a much better look-out.

More canvas was put on, although the masts of the Revenge were already bending like reeds beneath the pressure.

The rate at which the frigate tore along now was something tremendous.

Onward sped the stately vessel like a race-horse dashing the salt spray from her prow, as she clove through the foam-crested waves.

Larger and larger grew the speck.

"Hark!"

Our hero held up his hand.

Then there came a faint dull sound from the distance.

It was the report of a gun.

"By Jove," cried Captain Canon, "it is the pirate—I am sure of it, and possibly there is some other ship close by. If there is an engagement we shall stand a capital chance of capturing the rascal after all. Now then, lads, clear the deck and be ready for action. By thunder, when I come broadside to broadside with the rascal I will rake him fore and aft as sure as I am commander of his Britannic Majesty's frigate the Revenge."

The greatest activity was now exercised by all on board the frigate.

The guns were loaded—the ammunition got ready, and the small arms distributed.

Meanwhile the sounds of firing became louder and more distinct each moment.

Larger and larger, too, grew the white speck in the distance.

Captain Canon kept it well covered with his glass.

Suddenly he uttered an exclamation—

"Master Lionel!"

"Yes, sir."

"You know the Vampire well."

"Rather."

"Then just take a sight of that vessel we are gaining on so rapidly."

And he handed our hero his glass.

Lionel-of-the-Sea clapped it to his eye at once.

For the next few moments all eyes were fixed upon him intently.

Then, to the astonishment of all, our hero yielded to one of those wild bursts of enthusiasm in which he occasionally indulged.

"Hurrah—hurrah! Surely the time is come. Yes, the moment approaches, and I shall soon have my sword at the miscreant's throat! Hurrah! —hurrah."

"Hurrah!" shouted Hans.

And a mighty cheer the next moment broke from the entire crew.

"It is the Vampire, then?" said Captain Canon, inquiringly.

"Yes," replied our hero, who could hardly control his emotions at all. "Yes, it is the Vampire, and furthermore she is attacking another ship."

"Ah! That accounts for the firing."

"Exactly," cried Lionel-of-the-Sea. "And surely fortune smiles upon us. We shall be able to steal up unobserved, if the crew of the merchantman make anything like a resistance—and then—and then."

"Woe betide Captain Kydd, and his band of marauders."

By this time the excitement on board the Revenge was rapidly approaching fever heat.

Half an hour went by.

By the expiration of that time all could now be seen that was going on between the Vampire and the ill-fated vessel quite distinctly.

And by the aid of a glass the black flag could be seen fluttering over that scene of wholesale murder.

The bow-chaser of the Revenge was loaded and run out.

They were, however, yet too distant from the Vampire to reach her with a shot.

How long the moments seemed to be now!

How slow the progress of the frigate through the water!

And the Revenge was making better speed than she had ever done before.

CHAPTER XXVII.

CAPTAIN KYDD ASTONISHES THE PIRATES, AND AT THE SAME TIME AMAZES THE CREW OF THE REVENGE.

THE Revenge was one of the fastest ships in the British Navy.

In fact, it was on account of her remarkable sailing powers that the Revenge had been selected for the duty of sweeping the pirates from the seas.

Hitherto, however, she had been unable to come to close quarters with the light-heeled and saucy little schooner.

But now there seemed every possible chance of the Revenge coming up with the Vampire.

Captain Canon scarcely once removed his glass from the two vessels.

"Can you see the deck of the merchantman, sir?" inquired our hero.

"My God!" exclaimed Captain Canon, by way of reply. "It is horrible. The entire crew is butchered, and the wretches are already getting the spoil on to the deck, which is slippery with blood and covered with prostrate bodies. I do not think that all are quite dead yet, for a poor writhing wretch has just reared himself up on one arm and stretched out his hand imploringly."

"The poor fellow doubtless wants water," suggested Lionel-of-the-Sea.

Captain Canon uttered a cry of horror.

"Great heavens! What barbarity! A pirate —a Nubian, he seems—of gigantic proportions, has just struck the poor fellow's arm off with a sweep of his scimitar. Why the devil does he not kill him outright? He is still writhing on the deck."

A shudder ran round the group.

Horror and indignation were stamped on the faces of all, from the captain to the cabin-boy.

There was a very evident and unmistakable expression on each countenance too.

A look which boded ill to the pirates when the Revenge got yardarm to yardarm with the Vampire.

"Who is that black miscreant?" inquired Captain Canon of our hero. "He seems by his dress and manner to be an officer of some kind."

"Ah!" replied Lionel-of-the-Sea. "That is the first lieutenant, Nero. A more ferocious villain there has never been in the world. He is the devil's own brother."

"He shall swing from the yardarm ere the sun sets."

Lionel-of-the-Sea shook his head.

"You will have to shoot him down. The wretch fights like a fiend from the lower regions, and knows no fear of mortal man.

Again Captain Canon swept the deck of the San Josef with his glass.

"What unparalleled audacity," he said. "Hang me if the fellow is not bent on carrying off his booty under our very noses."

"Hurrah!"

A hearty cheer came from the crew of the Revenge.

"Another five minutes," said Mr. Marks, "and I think we shall be able to make a shot tell."

"In less time than that," cried Captain Canon. "Now then, bring that bow-chaser to bear on the rigging. Once crippled, and she is ours, lads, as sure as there is a sun in the sky."

The order was received with a loud cheer.

The bow-chaser was aimed with great care at the rigging of the Vampire.

The sailors crowded to the bulwarks, and watched with intense anxiety for the result of the shot.

Captain Canon gave the word.

A puff of white smoke jutted from the bow of the frigate.

Boom!

* * * * * *

The startling announcement made by Captain Kydd, that the Revenge was so close upon them, filled the pirates with consternation.

A rush and a scramble was at once made to regain the deck of the Vampire.

Captain Kydd's face flushed, and flashes of fury gleamed from his eyes.

"Hold—hold!" he roared, stamping his foot with rage. "Come back, you infernal cowards. Do you not know that partly on the deck, and partly in the hold of the San Josef there is gold—heaps of bright glittering gold that is worth upwards of a million pounds sterling."

"But—but the Revenge," gasped several of the crew who stood near.

"Hell take the Revenge!" thundered Captain Kydd. "The gold that is there we have bought with our blood, and that is the reason why I hurl my defiance at the frigate, and swear by heaven to have it—quick there, you lubbers, bear a hand here!"

The pirates were so thunderstruck at Captain Kydd's audacity, that for something over a second a profound hush came over the awful scene.

Then, with loud cries they rushed back and resumed their task of getting the gold up from the hold.

But the transferring of so much gold from one ship to another could not be accomplished in a minute, even by men used to such extraordinary exertions as the pirates.

Every instant they expected to hear the sullen roar of the frigate's opening fire.

Captain Kydd knew that the first shot would come the moment they were within the range of the frigate's guns.

"Now then, lads—look out," he said, suddenly. "Is there much more to be brought up? We shall have a shot in a minute or so."

"The last is on deck," panted a pirate, as he emerged from the hold of the San Josef, followed by several other picturesque ruffians, who were actually smoking with the heat occasioned by their extraordinary exertions.

"Hurrah!"

"Over with it there—quick! on your lives!—Ah! here it comes!"

As Captain Kydd spoke a cloud of smoke belched from the bows of the frigate.

Then the dull report of the distant gun boomed over the waves which rose and fell between.

Splash!

The heavy iron messenger dropped into the water about five yards astern of the Vampire.

"Whew!" whistled the pirate. "That looks like good shooting. Had that ball carried a little further it would have played the devil with our top hamper. Now then lads—back to the Vampire; there is not an instant to be lost."

Pell-mell they rushed to their ship, and bounded over the bulwarks with the agility of cats.

How they managed to alight on their feet is a mystery.

Some idea of what a scramble it must have been can be formed from the fact that in less than fifty seconds from the time the shot splashed into the water every one of the pirates was on board the Vampire.

"Off with the grapnels!"

These were instantly thrown off.

There was a rattling noise as the Vampire's yards swung round.

Up aloft into the rigging sprang the pirates, and with a rapidity truly wonderful the Vampire's white sails were bent to the breeze.

Boom!

There was a crash, and splinters flew over the stern gallery of the schooner.

The ball, however, did but little damage.

"Hurrah!" cried Captain Kydd, springing aft as the Vampire heeled half over and then commenced to fly through the waves like an arrow.

"The gold is ours, and we will slip them yet. Ha—ha!—what chance does that great bulky frigate stand of overhauling my beautiful and matchless craft !"

The pirates uttered a loud hurrah.

They had full confidence in the ability of their captain and the sailing powers of the Vampire.

The long brass gun, which we have before had occasion to mention, was now directed towards the frigate.

Captain Kydd superintended the working of the gun, which was most remarkable for the distance it would carry.

"Give me the link," cried Captain Kydd.

A piece of lighted tow was handed to him.

The pirate instantly applied it to the touch-hole.

There was a flash and a puff.

Then, as the report rang out, and the gun re-coiled, Captain Kydd stepped aside, and still holding the lighted link in his hand, waited for the result of his shot.

He laughed exultantly.

The frigate's bowsprit was injured by the shot which the sure eye and hand of the celebrated pirate had sent speeding with unerring aim across the foaming brine.

The damage done was sufficient to very greatly impede the progress of the frigate through the water for a time.

CHAPTER XXIX.

THE PIRATES' ISLAND.

MEANWHILE the saucy and light-heeled Vampire careered through the water at a rate which pro-mised soon to leave the frigate far behind.

The breeze was very strong, and the Vampire's masts bent like canes beneath the pressure of her white gleaming sails.

Nero, who took his stand near Captain Kydd, glanced upward with a doubtful eye.

"I say, captain," he remarked, "I think we had better take in a little canvas."

"Why !"

"See—the strain is so great, that each moment I expect to hear an ominous crash up aloft."

"Pooh," laughed Captain Kydd. "The Vam-pire's masts are strong as whalebone. Were the breeze still stiffer than it is, not one inch would I take in just now. See how merrily we dance along. An eagle on the wing is scarce more rapid in its flight."

And in good truth the schooner seemed to fly over the water at a rate which fully justified the assertion of the pirate captain.

Flauntingly the black flag, with its curious device, fluttered from the masthead, as if scouting the Revenge and inviting pursuit.

They were now once more beyond the reach of the frigate's terrible guns.

"Ha—ha !" laughed Captain Kydd. "'Twas right bravely done. We are clear of the Revenge, and we have the gold in our possession. Hurrah for a pirate's life !"

And he waved his sword aloft.

"Hurrah ! Hurrah ! Hurrah !"

From every throat went upward to the sky that wild, fierce, and exultant cheer.

The Vampire had just entered a small bay, and the scenery beyond was simply magnificent.

Although exceedingly small, the pirates' island was one of the most delightful ones on the western coast of Africa.

And being quite out of the ordinary track of vessels it was—as Lionel-of-the-Sea had stated to Captain Canon—wholly unknown to anyone but Captain Kydd and the crew of the Vampire.

The bay was sufficiently deep to allow the schooner to approach quite close to the shore.

The anchor was dropped.

Bang !

Loud and clear upon the air rang the report of a musket.

That was a signal from one of the sentries on the shore that the Vampire had returned.

It was answered by several more shots in different directions.

Almost immediately, a number of swart fierce-looking rascals, all armed to the teeth, appeared on the beach.

"Hurrah for Captain Kydd !"

The cheer was replied to right heartily by those who swarmed on the deck of the Vampire.

Then the boats were lowered.

A hearty welcome awaited the returned pirates from their friends on the island.

Captain Kydd took his seat beside his beautiful bride, Zulu, in the gig, and was rowed ashore.

He was greeted by a deafening cheer as he sprang on to the beach.

"Hurrah for Captain Kydd !"

That was the shout to which the lusty lungs of the pirates gave vent.

"And three cheers for the pirate queen," cried Captain Kydd. "Look you, comrades all—I've brought another treasure to our island. The gold is not all I have won. Here is a woman who will win as much of your esteem, and render you as many services as I have done. She is a dove in a cote and a demon in the fray. Hurrah for the pirate queen !"

If the cheers had been lusty before, they were deafening now, as the pirates, taking off their caps, crowded round Kydd and his bride.

Zulu received their homage with a majestic grace that would have filled many a European Queen with envy.

The men stopped.

"I have been thinking," said Kydd to Nero, "that it will be quite as well to bury this gold in a fresh place."

"Just so, captain. And where do you propose that spot shall be ?"

"In the centre of those six palms which grow almost in a circle."

"What, in the forest yonder ?"

"Yes."

"A better place could not be, but you must make a memorandum of the fact in your log—or —or——"

"Or what?"

"You might forget, or—or we might forget where the treasure is hidden."

"Pah," and Kydd made a gesture of contempt. "I never forget. Why don't you speak out like a man, and say, we have not the greatest confidence in our own memories, and you may meet your death at any moment, and therefore it behoves us to be careful."

Nero grinned.

"That's so like you, Captain Kydd."

"I hate meek-mouthed people," replied the pirate captain. "But come along and let us hide the treasure. I'll record the fact, never fear. I never fail to do that."

CHAPTER XXX.

THE ATTACK ON THE PIRATES' ISLE—THE STORM —THE PHANTOM SHIP—NEW PERILS.

CAPTAIN KYDD led the way towards the forest.

Nero and the others followed with the spoil of the San Josef.

Into the very middle of the forest they forced their way, nor did Captain Kydd pause until he reached a rather open spot, where six stately palm-trees grew in a circle.

The pirates were provided with spades.

They set to work with characteristic energy, and quickly made a deep hole in the ground.

"Now then, bear a hand here," cried one of the pirates, seizing one of the handles of the iron-bound chest. "In it goes."

Several of the pirates sprang to his assistance.

But before the huge chest was raised from the ground, all recoiled and looked blankly in one another's faces.

"What is that?" demanded Captain Kydd.

The roar of artillery echoed through the forest.

Captain Kydd was thunderstruck.

The pirates exchanged glances of alarm and amazement.

Boom—boom—boom.

"The Revenge!" cried Captain Kydd.

Shots and shells were poured upon the island so thickly, that they could not fail to commit much havoc.

Every minute bombs were bursting in the air.

As for the Revenge, all that could be seen of her was the smoke of her guns, which completely enveloped her.

"Nero!"

"Here, captain."

And the sable pirate stepped to his side.

"Quick for your life! If the Vampire is sunk we shall be ruined. Take a crew on board and defend her to the last. I leave her to your charge entirely. Meanwhile I will endeavour to silence those infernal guns. Now 'smart's' the word."

"Aye-aye, captain."

Nero waited for no more, but made his way to the beach by a path down which few would have ventured, shouting out

To the boats! The Vampire is in danger!"

"And if you are brave men, you will silence those guns," cried Zulu, as she turned to the swarthy captain, who had watched her with admiration.

With wonderful expedition the boats were launched.

Into them the pirates bounded like so many cats, and a cheer came from their comrades on shore as they rowed off to the schooner.

But if Nero was prompt and energetic in his action, Captain Kydd was still more so.

He kissed his bride, put her aside, and, with the speed of an antelope, made his way to the batteries, where the guns were already being worked.

The pirates who stood round the black and sullen cannon, with flaring links in their hands, greeted him with a shout.

"Hurrah for Captain Kydd."

"Is the Revenge well covered?"

And he glanced across the bay.

"Aye-aye."

"Then let them have it, lads."

No sooner was the order given than executed.

There was a succession of red and vivid flashes along the rattling rocks and cliffs—a long rolling cloud of smoke and a roar like that of thunder, only louder, deeper and more alarming.

Then a sudden breathless silence sounded.

The smoke of the battery rolled away.

Eagerly every eye was strained towards the Revenge.

She, too, became visible now, and as the wind cleared the "death-shade" from her magnificent hull with its triple row of teeth and her tall tapering masts, a lusty cheer awoke the echoes around.

So accurate had been the aim of the pirates— and so great was the devastation wrought on board the Revenge, that for the time at least her guns were silenced.

But for the time only.

Again the guns of the mettlesome frigate poured forth their thunder and smoke.

And again did the pirates return the fire.

This time, however, but little damage was done by either.

In the first place, the pirates were snugly ensconced behind the rocks, and in the second the frigate thought proper to shift her position the moment she had delivered her broadside.

"Bravo!" cried Captain Kydd, "Bravo! Did I not tell you we could hold our own if we did but exert ourselves! Ha, ha, ha!"

"May I be keel-hauled," exclaimed a pirate of most ferocious aspect, "if the infernal frigate aint had enough of it— why she's sheering off."

Captain Kydd smiled grimly, but shook his head.

"I'd rather she didn't sheer off. I think I understand what her movements mean."

The men regarded him apprehensively.

"What is it, captain?"

"Why you see," explained Captain Kydd, "They've had enough of our batteries for the present——"

"Hurrah!"

"But I would rather they had waited so that we could have blown them clean out of the water," Captain Kydd went on. "For, you see, by merely getting beyond the reach of our guns and then dropping anchor they place us in a somewhat awkward position."

"Ah!"

"To get the Vampire out of the bay will be by no means an easy or an unperilous undertaking while the frigate is lying in wait just beyond."

"No—no," responded the pirates in chorus.

"And what is to prevent Captain Canon from quitting these waters for what you may term a few hours and sending a message home which would result in the fitting out of a whole squadron?"

To these queries the pirates made no reply.

They recognised the full force of their captain's argument.

"Never mind, lads—I only show you the true position of affairs. You leave all to me, and as sure as my name is Kydd I'll bring you out of the difficulty as nicely as possible. Remember this—be true to one another and obey my orders with the greatest possible promptitude, and all will turn out well. Forget it, and I will not be answerable for the consequences."

It was by making such speeches on such occasions that Captain Kydd maintained his influence over the wild and lawless men who had vowed to follow his fortunes to the death.

Thus it was he inspired them with a vast amount of respect and dread.

And now let us see what the Revenge is about.

The frigate was steering off in a south-westerly direction.

Captain Kydd placed his glass to his eye.

Long and steadily he looked.

As he did so the colour faded from his cheeks.

His eyes seemed starting from their sockets.

His hands shook violently. the glass falling from his nerveless grasp to the rocks upon which he stood.

The pirate captain staggered back as if some one had smitten him between the eyes.

"Great heaven!" he gasped. "It surely cannot be—and yet—and yet—let me think."

Captain Kydd clapped his hands to his brow, and bent his head in thought.

The pirates regarded their leader with no small amount of uneasiness.

Why had this sudden change taken place in him?

Recovering his self-possession by one of those almost superhuman efforts which only such men are capable of, he stooped and picked up the glass.

Then he took a step forward and raised the glass again.

With a yell Kydd suddenly hurled the glass from him, and as he did so his face grew black as night, while white foam flew before the words he yelled rather than shouted.

"Ten thousand curses! Thwarted! Thwarted! Thwarted!—I see it all now. Oh, what a fool I have been. Only let me come within arm's length of him again and by the fiends he shall not quit my sight with life! Nero—ho—ho—Nero!"

And placing his hands to his mouth he shouted for his lieutenant in a stentorian voice.

One of the pirates advanced and touched his forelock.

"Excuse me, captain, but Nero has gone to look after the Vampire."

"Ah! So he has! I—I had forgotten."

"Well, captain, who shall wait on you? May we make so bold as to ask if anything very serious is about to happen."

Captain Kydd drew a long breath.

"All has gone well so far—look you, lads! I am going to see how things stand on board the Vampire. In the meantime see that a bright look-out is kept all round the island,for it is impossible to tell at which point the next attack will be made."

Kydd descended to the beach.

Several of the pirates followed closely in his footsteps.

The gig was then launched, and in it Captain Kydd proceeded to the Vampire.

He was received on deck with a shout of joy

The pirate laid his hand upon the black lieutenant's shoulder.

"Nero!"

"Yes, captain."

"The Revenge did not discover us by chance, as i at first surmised."

"No. I thought it strange that she should drop upon us in that manner. But surely, captain, there is not a traitor amongst us. If so, by——"

"No, no," explained Kydd, hurriedly, "it is not that; it is no such traitor as you suspect who has betrayed us. He who has brought the Philistines upon us had a perfect right, which even I cannot deny, to do so when he had the power. Ah! how furious it makes me to think what a fool I was. I ought to have blown his brains out with my own hand. But never again will I commit a like blunder. So swears Captain Kydd the pirate."

"What mean you, captain?" demanded Nero, "you speak in enigmas, and I am a poor hand at a puzzle! Who is it that has betrayed us?"

"LIONEL-OF-THE-SEA!"

Nero staggered back.

"L-Lionel-of-the-Sea?" he gasped.

"Even so," replied the pirate captain. "He is at this moment on board the frigate."

"Ah, captain, you should have taken my advice at the time. Believe me, the best method of getting rid of your enemies is to draw a knife or a pistol, and so settle the matter at once and for ever. But what is the next move? I'll wager you've made up your mind in regard to that already, in spite of the particularly puzzling character of our present position."

Captain Kydd smiled in his odd way.

The celebrated pirate was by no means unsusceptible of a little flattery at times.

That is, if it was conveyed to him in a delicate manner.

"Well, I suppose, Nero, you understand our position now, as well as I do."

"Or nearly so," replied the black, "and therefore I was at a loss to know how you mean to extricate yourself and us from a difficulty of such an overwhelming kind."

"We have only one chance, Nero, and that is a truly desperate one."

"And what is that?"

"To-night, unless I am very much mistaken, we shall have some roughish weather. Of this we must take advantage."

"In what way, captain?"

"Why, by giving the frigate the slip."

"But the island, captain, and the treasure."

"Ha, ha! You surely do not think I have the slightest idea of abandoning them altogether. No, no, Nero. What I propose to do is this. Leave a sufficiently strong garrison on the island to hold it until we can return."

"Return!"

"Yes, return. In fine, I intend to come back as quietly as possible, and perhaps we shall be able to sink the frigate, and then, once more the existence of our island will be a secret, shared only by the followers of Captain Kydd, ha, ha!"

And the pirate rubbed his hands gleefully at the prospect of being able to send the noble frigate and her five hundred fearless hearts to the bottom of the South Atlantic, there to lie until the sea shall give up its dead.

"But how?" demanded Nero. "How on earth can you hope to cope successfully with such a vessel as the Revenge?"

"Were she not an English frigate," replied the pirate captain, with a laugh, "I would, single-handed as we are at present, risk an encounter with her; but as it is I deem it necessary to obtain some assistance."

"Ah." Nero jumped at the idea.

"But," he inquired, after a pause, "what assistance could we get?"

"As much as we require," answered the pirate. "Paul Jones and Captain Kydd together would prove themselves, I fancy, a match for the finest frigate afloat in these or any other waters."

"Paul Jones," echoed Nero. "Surely you do not know Paul Jones?"

"Know him! Ha—ha—ha—! Why, it is five years ago since we first met, and then we fought from noon until sunset."

All this while Captain Kydd had been attentively watching the sky.

The signs which he observed were perfectly satisfactory.

The night, which was now rapidly approaching, promised indeed to be a dark and tempestuous one.

Black and threatening clouds hovered in the distance, and ominous sounds came from afar, caused by the soughing of the wind.

By this time, all that could be seen of the Revenge was a white speck—so small, that even the piercing and practised eye of Captain Kydd could scarcely discern it.

But there, in that one spot, she remained.

Captain Kydd watched it for two hours, and saw not the least alteration in its position.

The Revenge was indeed lying in wait.

Stationed where she was, it would be impossible for the Vampire to leave the bay without being seen by those on the look-out, excepting under cover of the night.

After a little more conversation with Nero, Captain Kydd went ashore again.

The sun had already set, and a deep gloom was creeping over the South Atlantic, the green waves of which gave forth a sullen roar as long lines of phosphorescent light flashed over their threatening crests.

Indeed there seemed little doubt but that it would prove an extremely dirty night.

A light burning in the watch-tower glimmered before him.

He hastened towards the steps, but ere he could reach them the graceful figure of Zulu appeared at the front of them.

The next moment she was clasped to his heart.

"Come," cried Captain Kydd, "dearest Zulu. A pirate's bride will surely never shrink from the tempest? Come; we must to sea again."

Zulu sighed softly.

But the regret she thus expressed at having to leave the beautiful island so soon, and which after all was only natural, was instantly—at least to all appearance—banished from her heart.

"The Vampire," she said. "Yes, I know. Bang—bang—boom—fight!"

And nodding her head to let him know what she expected was coming, she drew her sword and flourished it fiercely in the air.

"Ha, ha, ha!" laughed Captain Kydd. "I verily believe the smell of sulphur is as sweet to your nostrils, Zulu, as was the odour of roses to your Southern mother."

Zulu regarded him with a puzzled air.

Her knowledge of English was not extensive enough to enable her to comprehend his meaning.

"Hark!"

Captain Kydd held up his hand, and assumed a listening attitude.

Very faintly he heard the muttering of thunder in the distance, and a grim smile lit up his face.

"We will lose not a minute," he said. "It is now quite dark enough, and I should like to get fairly out on the ocean by the time the tempest bursts."

Leading his bride to the beach, the Rover lifted her into the gig, and then got in himself.

They were soon on board the Vampire.

Captain Kydd sent Zulu into the cabin and shut the door.

Now all was bustle and activity on board the pirate.

Smartly some of the men tramped round at the capstan while their comrades busied themselves with setting such sails as Captain Kydd deemed prudent.

The wind was blowing stiffly from the south-west, and in a very short time the Vampire was cutting through the water at a great rate.

And now, from out of the dense blackness overhead, the red forked lightning came streaming down, lighting up the hissing brine into which it descended for a brief interval, which was followed by seemingly denser darkness and rattling peals of thunder, which mingled terribly with the clash and roar of the raving waves.

And at every flash did Captain Kydd glance in the direction in which he thought the frigate was.

But not a trace of her did he see.

SUDDENLY there came one broad bright blaze of electric light which flickered over the surface of the ocean for several seconds, at the very time when the Vampire was on the top of one of the highest waves it had yet climbed.

Captain Kydd uttered a shout, but it was drowned in the clamour of the tempest.

Clearly and distinctly he saw the great hull and mighty masts of the Revenge.

And, furthermore, she was most surely in their track.

Whether those on board the frigate were aware of the fact or not he could not say.

But certain it was that the frigate was following dead in their wake.

Captain Kydd seized his speaking trumpet.

The wind had by this time fallen greatly.

But still the frigate's poles were quite bare.

" The Revenge—the Revenge !" he shouted.

He was answered by a hoarse cry.

"Who'll go aloft," yelled Captain Kydd, "and spread a sail or two ?"

There was a slight hesitation on the part of the men.

The duty was perilous indeed.

" I tell you," roared Captain Kydd, " that unless some of you run the risk we shall all perish. The Revenge is close upon us, and directly in our wake."

There was a slight discussion.

Then several of the most reckless of the pirates sprang aloft to do a deed from which the boldest sailor might well have shrank.

They had faith, however, in Captain Kydd, and believed, therefore, that the Vampire would be able to carry a little canvas even in such a storm as that.

It was indeed a daring experiment.

The sails were bent.

For a moment the Vampire staggered and seemed in peril of capsizing.

Then, like a hound let loose from the leash, she started forward with creaking boards and timbers, which groaned and quivered in a most alarming way.

The masts bent like whalebone.

But on—on sped the pirates' bark, and as she bounded over the foaming and roaring billows, Captain Kydd gave vent to his glee in a perfect shriek of triumphant joy, which made itself heard above the hundred and one deafening sounds which rendered night so hideous.

" Safe !" screamed Captain Kydd, " safe, the fiends ! The danger is past. Hurrah !"

In the midst of the tempest the high-pitched voice of the pirate captain sounded strangely unnatural.

But the crew responded not to the cheer, if cheer it could be called.

" The danger is passed," yelled Captain Kydd again. " Hurrah !"

Nero came staggering up, although it was both difficult and dangerous for anyone to move about the deck of the schooner at that moment.

" Captain."

" What now ?"

" How much longer will this storm continue ?"

" I cannot possibly tell," replied Kydd. " But such tempests in these latitudes are seldom of any duration. In less than half an hour all traces of the storm may have completely disappeared."

" We have had a dreadful time of it."

" You speak truly."

The negro growled something under his breath and made his way forward again with considerable difficulty.

Captain Kydd was, however, too excited at that moment to notice anything strange in his lieutenant's demeanour.

But had he been in a calmer and more collected mood Captain Kydd's piercing eyes would not have failed to read danger in the look which the negro gave him as he glided away.

* * * * * *

The storm had subsided.

The sea, however, was still rolling high, and the weather was exceedingly dirty.

But without sustaining the slightest injury, the pirate ship had weathered the storm, and now she careered gallantly on her way.

The wind had fallen, and so more canvas was spread, until her dark and sweeping hull tore through the waters at a most amazing rate.

Now that all immediate danger was over Captain Kydd retired to his cabin.

And surely, in all conscience, the pirate captain needed a little repose.

Shortly afterwards Nero also quitted the deck.

He made his way to the fore cabin.

Pushing open the door he strode in.

He was received with a faint cheer.

This issued from the throats of several sombre-looking pirates, who were gloomily gathered round the table.

Evidently these ruffians had been discussing a matter of the gravest importance, for each brow was bent in thought and each visage wore an unusually grave expression.

There was something threatening too in the manner in which they clutched the hilts of their daggers, kreeses, and cutlasses.

Nero held up his hand, and the cheer subsided.

The black carefully closed the door after him, and shot the little brass bolts at the top and at the bottom into their sockets.

" Well, comrades," he said in a low voice ; " so

LIONEL OF THE SEA.

far all goes well. The captain has retired to rest."

"And a good job if he never rises any more," muttered a black-bearded ruffian.

"Aye!" put in another. "Would I were at his side. I'd slice his throat as if it were an onion."

"Right, comrades," put in a third, huskily. "And something of the kind must be done, or, depend upon it, we are all doomed men."

"Aye, aye," muttered another at the foot of the table. "While the captain is on board there is not one of us who is safe for a moment!"

"Stop in a haunted ship I will not, and that's flat," broke in the first speaker, with characteristic abruptness.

"It's only Kydd the phantom troubles himself about," said Nero. "And you may depend that were he disposed of we should see no more of Vanderdecken and his spectral bark."

"Ah!"

The sound of a deep and simultaneous inspiration ran round the board.

"What think you, comrades?" inquired Nero, as he glanced round from one to the other.

"We think with you," was the reply.

"Good!" exclaimed the negro. "And are you willing to place yourselves under my command, and to obey me in future as implicitly as you have hitherto obeyed Captain Kydd?"

"We are," was the unanimous response.

"Then all will be well!"

And the whites of the negro's eyes gleamed horribly in the sickly glare of the oil-lamp suspended from the cabin roof.

There was another suppressed cheer.

"Hurrah for Nero! Three cheers for the new commander of the Vampire!"

Goblets were charged with grog and drained to the dregs by the conspirators.

And Nero had to warn them into silence.

"Hush! Hush!" he cried. "You forget that our scheme is yet in its infancy—

"Aye! aye!" murmured the others. "Let us know what it is you propose to do?"

"Very well, comrades. You have only to listen and I will explain."

"We'll listen."

"In the first place, then," said Nero, "what I I propose to do is to seize the ship—put the captain to death, and likewise all those thick-headed and obstinate fools who refuse to join us in the enterprise."

"But when?" inquired the man with the beard —"but when do we set to work?"

"At once," replied Nero.

"At once?"

"This very hour," replied the black, who knew it was wise to strike while the iron was hot. "You must not forget, lads, that every moment of delay is a moment of danger to all. Captain Kydd still remains on board. So long as he does so the Vampire is in peril."

The pirates sprang to their feet.

Their superstitious fears had been wrought to such a pitch that they would have rushed pell-mell to the state-cabin with naked weapons in their hands, and there and then have made an assault upon Captain Kydd.

But Nero restrained them.

Full well did the wily negro know the cool, daring spirit of the man they were about to attack, and how more than likely it was that under such circumstance he would find some means of thwarting them.

Therefore he waved the mutineers back with his hand.

"Patience—patience!" he cried. "You will ruin all.

"The next thing to be done," said Nero, "is to ascertain as quickly as possible the feelings of our comrades, and to mark those who are still determined to stand by Kydd."

"Aye, aye!"

The crew tumbled up on deck.

It was now broad daylight.

The mutineers now set to work to ascertain the sentiments of their comrades.

They met with great success.

The same feeling which animated them was rife throughout the ship.

Indeed, things began to look very bad for Captain Kydd.

There were a few, of course, to whom the mutineers were afraid to make overtures.

And these were left to take their chance.

Their fates rested in their own hands.

The mutineers were careful not to raise the least alarm.

Gradually they collected in a body outside the door of the state-cabin.

Lots were drawn as to who should be the one to enter first.

Black Bill was the man fated to do this duty.

He seized the handle, and turned it as softly as possible.

The others crouched close upon his heels, with naked cutlasses gleaming and bristling in their hands.

"Now then," cried Nero, "look sharp—what are you afraid of?"

"Nothing," retorted Black Bill, as he flung open the door.

As he did so, there was a flash and a bang.

Black Bill gave a shriek, and staggering backward several paces, fell heavily.

The smoke was whirled rapidly away by the wind, and there, with his form drawn to its full height and a long-barrelled pistol in each hand, stood Captain Kydd himself.

The mutineers shrank back.

There was something in the pirate's aspect which cowed them.

Even Nero quailed before the eagle-like glance he swept around.

CHAPTER XXXIV.

HOW CAPTAIN KYDD SUPPRESSED THE MUTINY
AND HOW HE TREATED NERO AFTERWARDS.

"WHAT is the meaning of this?" demanded Captain Kydd. "Who will be the next?"

Yes, there stood Captain Kydd in the doorway of his cabin, with his form drawn up to its full height.

A blaze of defiance came from his eyes.

There was danger in the very set of his teeth and the curve of his upper lip.

From the muzzle of the pistol he had just discharged a thin wreath of blue smoke was still curling.

"Speak!" cried the pirate captain again. "What is the meaning of all this, and who will be the next?"

Nero's face puckered up in all the hideousness of an angry ape, and, suddenly flinging himself upon Captain Kydd, bore him heavily down.

A yell of triumph burst from the pirates' lips.

Nero's act was an unexpected stroke of good fortune, and they shouted for very glee.

In less time than it takes to record it, Captain Kydd was securely bound, and the black lieutenant stood over him, his eyes glaring furiously, and his lips moving mockingly.

"I am captain of the Vampire now," he said, "and you must beg your life of me."

"Never, you dusky scoundrel," Captain Kydd hissed through his foaming lips. "Never, you white-livered, ungrateful hound!"

"Land ho!" shouted the man on the look-out.

"Where away?"

"About ten miles north nor'-west."

"Nothing could be better," Nero said, grimly. "As we do not want any prisoners on board the Vampire, we will take the liberty of leaving Captain Kydd behind for a change, so that he may enjoy a little quietude."

What ho, there! Place him in irons and stand by to lower a boat."

The pirate chief was almost purple with rage, and the veins on his forehead stood out like whipcord.

"I will have revenge," he said, "and it will be all the sweeter for waiting a little time for it."

"Silence," Nero said, drawing a jewelled-hilted dagger from his sash. "You look angry and virtuous now that you cannot help yourself. Bah! If my hands are stained with blood, you have waded knee-deep in it."

Captain Kydd made no reply, but he bit his under lip until it grew ghastly white.

"Now then," said Nero, "keep your ears open, lads, to take my orders. Where is that woman, Zulu? We will put her on shore as well, and leave her to look out for a passing vessel."

"Scoundrel!" said Captain Kydd. "If there's no spark of mercy in your heart for me, have pity on a defenceless woman."

"As much pity as you have shown to thousands of her sex," Nero replied. "The island, no doubt, is a fruitful one, and she will be able to exist. In that respect she will be luckier than you, for if there is a dungeon in yonder fortress I intend to make you safe within it."

"And leave me to starve?"

"Of course," Nero replied, with savage brutality. "Don't think for a moment that I am going to waste rations on such a dog as you."

In reply to a signal from the black lieutenant two of the pirates went below, and presently returned with Zulu between them.

They had taken her by surprise.

"Unhand me, wretches!" she cried. "Mark well my words. You will bitterly repent of your conduct towards the captain. Whatever his fate may be I will share it."

Captain Kydd gave her a grateful smile.

"Nay," Nero said, "I fear that I must separate you. You shall be as free as the air, and if you can rescue your beloved husband, that will be a matter for you. I wish you luck. Lower away there. The sooner we unship this rubbish from the Vampire the better for everybody."

The boat was made ready in a very short space of time, and eight men stepped into it.

They were quickly followed by Nero and the prisoners.

"Give way there!" shouted the new captain of the Vampire.

In half an hour the keel grated on the sand, and Nero was the first to land.

"We have had enough talk," he said, "so the best thing we can do is to say no more, but part friends."

"Friends!" Captain Kydd repeated, as his brow grew as dark as a rising thunder-cloud; time will prove what kind of a friend I am to you."

Nero laughed ironically.

"Nothing seems to please you," he said. "You take fair and foul words alike. Ha! I am not mistaken in yonder place. It was a Spanish fortress, and doubtless contains just the sort of lodgings I think will suit you splendidly. Zulu will remain here to enjoy the fine balmy air. If she attempts to follow us I shall be reluctantly compelled to stop her progress with a bullet."

"You are very kind," Zulu returned, with a mocking sneer. "I will do as you wish, and find means of settling accounts with you at some other time."

So saying, she sat down under a tree, and the pirates led Captain Kydd away.

The fortress, old as it was, still remained in a fair state of preservation, and Nero having descended a deep flight of stairs, and discovered a dark, gloomy dungeon, ordered Captain Kydd to be thrust into it.

"Farewell, Captain Kydd," Nero shouted. "I dare say you will find yourself rather lonely, but you can pass the time away by thinking over the past."

The pirate chief had received a severe blow when Nero threw him, and a handkerchief had been twisted round his head.

When left alone he sat for some time, wondering whether what had happened could be true. The mutiny, his sudden downfall and imprisonment, had come so sudden that all seemed like a dream.

At length he called out whether he was to perish of hunger and thirst.

The sound of his voice was answered by another.

"Take courage," Zulu said, through the grating, "I have found means to save you."

"Yes," Captain Kydd replied, "but we must both starve on this wretched island."

"No, no," said Zulu, "we will be on board the Vampire an hour after dark. Keep away from the grating, I am going to break it open."

Captain Kydd knew that Zulu was a wonderful woman, but he could hardly credit that she had discovered means to escape in so short a time what had promised to be a lingering and awful death.

The pirate's bride had torn down a stout branch of a tree, and using it as a lever easily forced the old rusty bars.

Then she, uttering a joyous cry, leaped into the dungeon, and drawing a file from a fold in her dress, soon liberated Captain Kydd from the irons.

"Follow me," she said, triumphantly. "As I was walking about the island I came upon a creek, and then right before my eyes lay a small boat sunk, so as to keep the planks from expanding under the sun's rays. It must have been left here by some ship's crew, perhaps by——"

"A brother pirate," Captain Kydd interposed. "But, Zulu, what are we to do for oars. We can't expect the boat to float up to the Vampire just to oblige us."

"You foolish man," she replied. "If a branch can burst thick bars asunder, surely we can find something of a similar material to do duty for oars."

"You are right, you always are," Captain Kydd said.

When darkness fell the creek was visited, and the work of drawing the boat out commenced. The labour proved a difficult one, but it was accomplished at last.

And then silently the boat drifted towards the Vampire, now the scene of revelry and gambling.

The presence of Captain Kydd was not observed until he stood on deck with Zulu at his side.

Amazed at their sudden appearance, the pirates started to their feet, and then shrank back in a body.

Like wild beasts in the presence of their keeper they stood before the man who had escaped their vengeance.

A scornful laugh broke from the lips of the Rover.

"Fools," he cried, "see what you have done for yourselves. No dungeon walls ever built can hold me fast. You sought my life, but you dare not take it."

As he spoke he seized the nearest man by the throat, and snatched a brace of pistols from his belt.

"Now come," he said. "By the black flag that waves above us you shall see how dearly I can sell my life, even against fearful odds. Zulu!"

She sprung forward, and, picking up a curved sword, flourished it defiantly over her head.

The mutineers inhaled a deep breath, and looked in one another's faces.

Captain Kydd saw that he had made an impression on all save one.

And that one was Nero.

The black had not, by any look or motion, indicated that he had ever listened to his captain's words.

He still kept his face averted—still kept his fingers coiled convulsively round the trigger of his pistol.

"That is not all," Captain Kydd went on. "In three weeks I say all this would assuredly happen; but I have not yet mentioned one other event that would be equally certain to take place, and in all human probability in a much shorter period, and that is, the capture of the Vampire and her crew. If you think I misrepresent matters, or that there is anyone else on board better able to take the command, tell me his name."

"No, no !" cried the mutineers.

"Hurrah for Captain Kydd !" cried one of their number. "Hurrah for Captain Kydd !"

"Hurrah for Captain Kydd !" shouted several others.

And then the cry was taken up and loudly was it vociferated throughout the Vampire.

"Hurrah for Captain Kydd."

The pirate captain restored one of the pistols to his belt, when he saw the caps waving in the air and heard the shout.

As he did so, Nero, with a yell like that of a wild beast, sprang towards him.

Bang !

Captain Kydd's hat flew off, and he himself staggered back.

Scarcely had the sound died away, when another report rang out.

It was succeeded by a hearty curse, and Nero's pistol fell from his nerveless grasp.

As it did so his left arm dropped powerless to his side.

That second shot was fired by Zulu.

At the same moment there was a universal shout.

All thought that Nero's shot had taken effect.

Even Captain Kydd fancied that he was wounded.

Such, however, was not the case.

The bullet had merely passed through his hat, but the shot had been sufficient to stagger him for the moment, on account of the closeness of Nero's aim.

Indeed, the pirate captain was, for the moment, half-blinded by the flash.

He actually felt his brow scorched.

But, by a most miraculous and almost unaccountable accident, the bullet went barely a quarter of an inch too high.

The pirate captain, however was scarcely two seconds in discovering that he had not been even so much as grazed by the mutineer's bullet.

"Ha! Villain—wretch, what would you do?" thundered Kydd.

And, with a bound like that of a tiger, he sprang upon the baffled pirate, and clutched him by the throat.

Nero struggled for an instant, and then went backwards on the deck with a crash sufficient to very nearly break every bone in his body.

"Attempt to rise," cried Kydd, "and I'll scatter your brains upon the deck."

He held the undischarged pistol in a direct line with the Negro's left eye.

Nero scowled at him with intense hatred.

"Cry quarter, said Kydd, "and I will spare you for the present. Remain silent for one minute, and you shall never speak again. When Captain Kydd fires, Nero, he never misses his mark!"

This biting remark was made in a loud and distinct voice which reached every ear.

And there was not a man on board the Vampire who did not implicitly believe the assertion.

The men crowded nearer.

They knew well the black lieutenant's proud, fierce spirit, and some of them fully expected to hear the crack of Captain Kydd's pistol, so confident did they feel that Nero would not sue for mercy.

But never were men more mistaken.

"The minute is nearly up," remarked Kydd.

And the cold glitter in his eyes showed that he would most certainly carry his threat into execution.

"Quarter!" cried Nero.

"Do you surrender?" demanded the pirate, without altering the direction of his barrel by a hair's breadth.

"Yes."

"Adams!"

"Aye, aye, sir," replied the boatswain.

"Clap Nero in irons, and keep him in the hold until I have decided what to do with him."

"Aye, aye, sir."

Cutlasses were drawn on all sides, and the next moment Nero was surrounded by the very men who a few hours before had declared themselves ready to stand by him to the last.

Captain Kydd maintained his stand on deck, pistol in hand, until Nero was marched away and safely stowed in the hold.

Then he returned the other pistol to his belt and glanced round at the crew with his old pleasant genial smile upon his face.

"Now, then, my lads," cried Captain Kydd, in a bluff, off-hand kind of way, "what is the grievance? You know very well that I'm not the man to refuse any reasonable request."

Then one of the mutineers stepped forward and touched his forelock.

He was a tall and powerful Englishman, with bronzed and weather-beaten countenance and a grizzled beard.

"Proceed, Jack. Get your jawing tackle in gear and go ahead."

"Well, d'ye see, Captain," continued Jack, "as I said afore, we like you, and should be sorry to lose you; but, damme, we can't stand—um—er——"

Jack was getting uneasy again.

"What?" demanded Captain Kydd, sharply.

"Ghosts!" said Jack with a shout. "There—there you've got it. The murder's out."

"Ghosts!" echoed Captain Kydd, who now guessed at once the real state of affairs. "Ha—ha—ha—what ghosts, pray?"

"What ghosts!" cried Jack. "Well, that's good too—what ghosts!—cuss me—why Vanderdecken and Co."

"Ha—ha—ha!"

Captain Kydd laughed heartily.

"And," cried several of the mariners who had pressed forward so as not to lose one word of this—to them important dialogue, "we know too that the appearance of the Flying Dutchman is a sign that our vessel is doomed."

"Tush!" exclaimed Captain Kydd. "I admit that such is generally the case. But we've seen the Flying Dutchman many times, and if the Vampire had been a doomed ship she would have gone to the bottom long ago."

"She may go at any moment."

"No," cried Captain Kydd, with a readiness of wit which did him credit. "The Vampire is safe, at least for the present, from this spectre ship, though if you had accomplished your purpose she would have gone down in less than twenty minutes."

"How's that, captain?"

Captain Kydd's reply caused a universal shout.

"I HAVE A COMPACT WITH VANDERDECKEN!"

CHAPTER XXXVI.

CAPTAIN KYDD AND NERO.

GREAT was the sensation created by this assertion.

A grim smile appeared upon the visage of the pirate captain.

Well did he know that there was nothing his superstitious crew would believe more readily than that he had made some strange and secret treaty with the spectre Vanderdecken.

Whatever uneasiness Captain Kydd had felt in regard to his own safety vanished completely now.

He felt confident that no one of the mutineers would again dream of raising a hand against him.

"Are you satisfied now?" demanded Captain Kydd.

"We are," chorussed the crew. "Three cheers for Captain Kydd! Hip, hip, hurrah!"

"Long live the Pirate Queen!" Jack cried

"Long live the Pirate Queen!" shouted the crew, enthusiastically.

And each man drank deeply.

Then Captain Kydd and Zulu withdrew.

Captain Kydd chuckled with glee as he returned to his cabin.

He had one or two matters of the greatest importance to weigh over in his mind.

There was the critical situation of the garrison on the island to be considered.

The best means of coming across Paul Jones, with as little loss of time as possible, to be thought of.

The fate of Nero to be considered.

These and a heterogeneous mass of other and scarcely less important matters occupied the mind of the pirate captain at that moment.

But the latter was the thing which chiefly engaged his attention just then.

Nero's fate trembled in the balance.

Captain Kydd was more than half-inclined to order him to be run up to the yardarm at once.

Had the culprit been any other than Nero he would instantly have been made an example of.

But the African was a most valuable man, and now the pirate captain knew the cause of the mutiny, and that he had nothing to fear from another outbreak of the same kind, he felt extremely reluctant to sacrifice his lieutenant.

"But what was he to do?"

That question puzzled Captain Kydd sorely.

After profound reflection he made up his mind as to the best course to adopt.

"Strike the gong, Zulu."

Zulu did as he requested.

The summons was instantly obeyed.

The door of the cabin was opened and the pirate on guard outside thrust in his head.

"Tell Jack Pyke to bring Nero before me at once."

"Aye—aye, sir."

The door closed.

Captain Kydd blew a few more clouds of smoke from his pipe.

Then there was a clatter of feet outside, and the next moment the tapping of a pistol-butt resounded on the panel.

"Come in," cried Kydd.

The door was thrown open and in marched Jack Pyke, followed by half a dozen ferocious-looking pirates, armed with naked cutlasses.

Nero was in their midst.

He was loaded with irons, but though he stood erect and maintained a certain air of defiance, there was a particularly wild look about his eyes, and he glanced furtively around.

Captain Kydd did not alter his position.

He simply turned his face towards the prisoner, and, sucking his pipe with a serene air of enjoyment, sternly regarded him.

Nero was trembling with concealed passion.

The air of supreme indifference assumed by Captain Kydd galled him exceedingly.

And, furthermore, he was not a little unnerved.

He knew that in such a mood Captain Kydd was most to be dreaded.

"I suppose," said Captain Kydd, looking straight into Nero's eyes, "you have not forgotten that one of the rules in our code is instantaneous death to the mutineer."

Nero glanced at him for a moment.

Then he drew his form so erect, in spite of the great weight of his fetters, that his chin was on a level with his custodian's cap.

"Hang me up," he said, laconically.

Captain Kydd eyed him narrowly.

But Nero withstood the searching glance.

Indeed, the air of supreme indifference he assumed was simply magnificent.

This was bringing matters to a crisis with a vengeance.

"Oh! you are tired of existence, I suppose?"

"Not quite," replied the negro.

"Still you long for a change of some kind. An alteration in your position, perhaps. You would like to be promoted to the rank of captain, would you not?"

Nero made no answer.

"Well, you cannot deny that you tried very hard to elevate yourself; but since you could not succeed without it, perhaps you will accept my assistance—I can have you elevated at once—placed high above myself."

"You mean you can raise me to the yardarm?"

"Most certainly."

"Well," remarked Nero, laconically, "one may as well be hung as drowned—"

"Now, I must admit you are a very brave and skilful man, Nero."

"And useful, too, sometimes," growled the black.

"Just so; therefore, in spite of the fact that you not only incited others to take my life, but actually fired upon me yourself, I should be very sorry to sentence you to death."

"Ah."

The negro drew a deep breath, and his eyes brightened.

"Now, Nero, what would you do if I were to order these irons to be struck off, and tell you to go about your duty as usual?"

For a moment Nero was utterly unable to reply.

Then Nero, though his arms were still held by the pirates on either side of him, took a step forward, and cried—

"Do it, Captain Kydd—do it, and never shall you repent the generous act. I swear it."

"You are free," replied Captain Kydd. "Now mind, I want no thanks—no assurances. Go—do your duty faithfully; fail not, or no fiend below endures more than you shall suffer on board the Vampire—Go!"

Captain Kydd pointed to the door.

Nero, loaded with chains, slunk out.

At the same moment the voice of the man at the masthead rang through the ship.

"Sail ho!"

Captain Kydd heard the hail, and instantly appeared on deck.

"Where away?"

"Off the starboard bow!"

Captain Kydd mounted to the quarter-deck and clapped his glass to his eye.

Nero at once took his place by the captain's side, as cool and unconcerned as if nothing had happened.

There was very little difficulty in making out the distant ship.

She was a large three-masted brig, with every rag of canvas spread, even to the stud-sails.

And she tore through the blue rippling waters at a tremendous rate.

Captain Kydd watched her movements attentively for several minutes.

Then he lowered his glass.

"Curse me," said Captain Kydd. "If that vessel is not flying from some pursuer I am a Dutchman."

In an instant the interest of the whole crew of the Vampire was aroused.

All eyes were turned towards the distant ship.

Nearer and nearer she came.

But no sign as yet could be discovered of her pursuer.

Suddenly, however, Captain Kydd uttered a cry.

"There she is! There she is! I told you all that the brig was being pursued, and, see, yonder is her pursuer."

Far away in the distance a white speck now became discernible.

To the crew of the Vampire it appeared like the wings of some large white bird hovering on the tops of the waves.

But with the aid of his glass Captain Kydd was able to make it out more distinctly.

It was a schooner with a low dark sweeping hull, and tall taper masts, which raked very much aft.

Who was the pursuer?

What other pirates had made their appearance in those waters?

Those were the questions which Captain Kydd was burning with impatience to solve.

A few more minutes and in all probability he would be able to tell.

How long those minutes seemed!

But at length the longed-for moment came.

* * * * * *

That terrific storm, which we have described in a previous chapter, was over, and the Revenge still breasted the heaving billows of the South Atlantic.

This fact, however, caused not the least surprise to her dauntless crew.

When the tempest was hushed the jolly tars lounged about, as was their wont, and if the events of the night were alluded to, it was in the most casual way, and with that air of indifference peculiar to British sailors.

Captain Canon, however, was by no means as good-tempered as was his wont.

The escape of the Vampire galled him exceedingly.

He had always flattered himself that he was one of the smartest commanders in the navy.

Therefore, to be baulked in such a manner by a scoundrelly pirate like Captain Kydd was annoying in the extreme.

What to do he scarcely knew.

His situation was a most peculiar one.

To attack the island would, in itself, be a most hazardous undertaking.

Captain Canon, however, did not for one moment doubt his ability to take it. but he knew that in order to do so much time and loss of life must inevitably ensue.

And in the meantime Captain Kydd would be at liberty to range about the ocean and pursue his career of blood and plunder unchecked.

And ought he to allow this?

That was the question which perplexed and harassed Captain Canon.

He would, without hesitation, have gone in chase of the pirate, but for one thing.

If he left his station, the wily pirate, having ascertained that fact, might easily enough return to the island, and remove his treasures to another place, and eventually elude him altogether.

Captain Canon paced his cabin with restless and irregular strides.

Suddenly he paused beside the table and struck upon a gong.

The marine on duty outside the door made his appearance at the entrance.

"Tell Master Lionel I wish to speak with him."

"Yes, sir."

The marine closed the door, and several moments elapsed.

Then our hero entered.

He was still attired in the picturesque costume he had worn on board the Vampire, and his long curling locks still fell about his shoulders in the old disordered way.

There was a trifle more colour on his cheeks, and a brighter light in his eyes, however, than when first Captain Canon saw him.

The commander of the Revenge was more impressed than ever with our hero's appearance.

"You sent for me, sir," said Lionel-of-the-Sea, looking at him full in the face.

"I did, boy—be seated."

With a graceful bow Lionel expressed his thanks for Captain Canon's civility, and took possession of one of those elegant gilt-backed chairs with which the state-cabin of the Revenge was furnished.

"I wish to speak to you about Captain Kydd."

"Any information I can give, or any other assistance I can render, you are more than welcome to, Captain Canon."

"You are, of course, well acquainted not only with Kydd's habits, but also with the island itself."

"I am indeed. There is not a foot of the island that is not as familiar to me as are the planks of the Revenge to you."

"Good."

"Do you think that Kydd will keep away from the island long, or is he likely to return at once?"

"Why, I feel sure he will slip back again as soon as he possibly can,' replied Lionel-of-the-Sea. "There is a loadstone there so strong that it will not fail to draw him swiftly back."

"And that loadstone?"

"A treasure—or rather treasures—gold and jewels in such quantities as no Emperor ever possessed. The untold wealth which Kydd has stored away on that island is fabulous. And do you think he will leave it long in jeopardy? No. Though he risks his life a thousand times, depend upon it the pirate will be back again sooner than you anticipate."

"I am glad you are so strongly of that opinion," cried Captain Canon, "because it sets my mind at rest. Now tell me, if you were in my place how would you act?"

"You do me great honour, Captain Canon."

"Not more than I think you deserve. From

"Is there anywhere in these latitudes another cruiser with whom you could consort?"

"Oh, yes! there is the Juno."

"Yes, to that also; but the difficulty is, that

"In the first place, I would attack and take possession of the island."

"That will be a long job."

"Yes! and one that will require a lot of fighting. The pirates now on shore will fight to the very last, and will prove themselves as fierce as tigers at bay."

"There is no question about that!"

"But before the attack is made upon the island, there is a craft which is very artfully concealed, and which the pirates use sometimes in taking merchandise to different foreign ports, where it is disposed of in the ordinary way of trade. This vessel is a little brigantine thing, built expressly for the purpose of traffic."

Now if we got possession of that craft?"

"It could easily be manned and sent with despatches to look after the Juno."

"By thunder!" exclaimed Captain Canon, enthusiastically. "That's the very thing. The difficulty is solved. I see it all. Lionel, my lad, you are a genius!

"To take possession of the brigantine will prove no easy nor unperilous task, I can assure you," said Lionel

"But seize it we will!" cried Captain Canon, emphatically.

"Most certainly! But the attempt must be made at the right moment, or the result may prove most disastrous."

"Of course—and where is this vessel?"

"Concealed, very artfully, behind some rocks at the north end of the island."

"Then what is to prevent us from steering to the place at once, and openly taking possession of it?"

Our hero smiled.

"You do not know these men with whom you have to deal so well as I do, Captain Canon. To

make for the north end of the island now would be at once to arouse their suspicions, and the batteries would open fire on us the moment we came within range."

"Just so."

"And if they suspected you of any designs against the brigantine, fire would immediately be opened upon her, and we should suffer the disappointment of seeing her sink."

"That is quite right. Your head is certainly screwed on the right way, Lionel. How do you propose to go to work?"

"Why, to wait until night, and then under cover of the darkness to make for the north end of the island, taking care all the time to keep out of the range of the battery in case of an accidental discovery."

"And what then?"

"Lower a boat, man it with Jack Tars, and give me the command. You shall have the brigantine then, come what will."

"Bravo, Lionel. I admire your spirit immensely. It shall be as you wish, and I can pay you no higher compliment than by expressing my intention to follow out your plan to the very letter. So now you had better go to your berth and get such rest as you can between now and the time to start on your night adventure."

* * * * *

"Ah! Now we shall see."

As he uttered this exclamation, Captain Kydd brought his glass to bear once more upon the strange schooner.

At the same moment a flag fluttered up to the masthead.

There was an almost breathless silence on board the Vampire as the massive folds of the flag spread out to the breeze.

Then to all the stars and stripes became apparent.

"Ha, ha!" cried Captain Kydd. "I fancied I could not be mistaken. It is as I thought—as I hoped. By Neptune! Nero, Fortune favours us once more."

The gigantic black looked inquiringly at the pirate captain.

The hasty and disjointed sentences to which Captain Kydd had given utterance were quite enigmatical to Nero.

"You know the schooner, now?"

"Know it!" echoed Kydd, with flushed cheeks and sparkling eyes—"of course I know it! Ha, ha! Who could have hoped for such a slice of luck? Scarcely have I expressed a wish to see Paul Jones, when, lo! he appears upon the scene as suddenly and as unexpectedly as if, at the utterance of some magic words, he had been brought hither by the geni of the deep."

"Paul Jones!" echoed Nero.

Like lightning the name of the celebrated freebooter passed from mouth to mouth, and a cheer resounded through the Vampire.

It was instantly suppressed.

Had the cheer reached the ears of those on board the fugitive brig they might have taken alarm at once, and there and then altered the course of their vessel.

Thus her capture, though none the less certain, would necessarily be materially delayed.

And Captain Kydd had no time to lose.

In fact the rover was burning with impatience to grasp Paul Jones once more by the hand, and furthermore, he felt that he should know not a moment's rest until he had successfully carried out his daring scheme for the relief of his men on the island, and the rescuing of his vast treasures from the threatened danger of falling into the hands of Captain Canon and his crew.

Therefore it may be judged with what anxiety he watched the movements of the schooner and the brig.

Both vessels were rapidly nearing the Vampire.

By this time, indeed, the latter was so close that had he been so disposed, Captain Kydd could have crippled her severely with his guns.

For this, however, there was not the slightest occasion.

Full sail the brig was careering towards them.

Evidently neither her captain nor her crew had the faintest suspicion of the real character of the Vampire.

CHAPTER XXXIX.

CAPTAIN KYDD AND PAUL JONES.

In ten minutes more they were actually side by side with the pirate, and with only a few fathoms of water between them.

A tarpaulin had been hung over the Vampire's stern, which effectually concealed her name.

By this time Captain Kydd had made the brig out to be a Frenchman, though no colours were flying.

"Ship ahoy?" cried Captain Kydd, with one hand to his mouth.

"A-a-hoy," came back the answering hail.

"What ship?" demanded the pirate.

"The brig, Aimée from Calais. We are pursued by Paul Jones—help us—for God's sake help us, or we shall all ha' butchered by pirates."

"Right," responded Kydd. "This is the John Bull of London. Come alongside, and curse me we'll give the Yankee such a licking as he never had before!"

The crew of the Aimée responded with a hearty cheer.

Never were men more cruelly deceived.

And now the sides of the Vampire and th bumped and grated together.

A cheer came from the deck of the Aimée.

The response was startling in the extreme.

Captain Kydd blew a loud blast upon his whistle.

"Vampire ahoy!" he cried, in a stentorian voice.

Then there issued from the throats of the pirates a hideous, fiendish, and appalling yell of triumph, as they bounded from their hiding places, and commenced swarming over the bulwarks of the doomed brig, with cutlasses flashing, knives gleaming, and pikes bristling in a most ferocious manner.

Exclamations of surprise, screams of terror, and yells of dismay ensued.

"Throw the grapnels," shouted Captain Kydd.

In an instant the order was obeyed.

The two vessels were securely locked together.

No words can convey the faintest idea of the fearful scene that ensued.

The crew of the Aimée were so thunderstricken, that at first they were wholly unable to offer the slightest resistance to the pirates, who shot and struck them down with as much ease as if they had been so many petrified figures.

One of the first to fall was the captain himself.

While the first fierce simultaneous yell of the pirates was ringing through the ships, and as the French captain was actually staggering back in amazement and horror, Nero leapt towards him, like some huge black hound, and seizing him by the throat plunged his sword to the hilt in his body.

Relentlessly the work of slaughter was done.

Meanwhile, what of the other schooner !

Captain Kydd had maintained his position on the quarter-deck of the Vampire in order to watch her movements.

From what he saw by the aid of his glass, Captain Kydd judged that his attack on the brig created almost as much astonishment on board the American privateer as it had done amongst the crew of the former.

Several of her sails were taken in, and, although she continued to approach, the speed of the schooner was much diminished.

"Ha ! ha ! ha !" laughed Kydd. " Paul Jones himself is bewildered, and approaches with caution. Let's give him a signal. Up with the Stars and Stripes."

The American flag was at once run up.

That Paul Jones understood perfectly what this meant was evident immediately.

A black flag was displayed by the schooner, and the sails which had been taken in were again unfurled.

A very few minutes sufficed to bring her close to the scene of strife.

If strife it could be called.

By this time the greater part of the unfortunate crew of the Aimée had been butchered.

Those who survived, however, fought desperately.

But one by one they succumbed to the pirates, who not only greatly outnumbered them, but who also were much more accustomed to the use of arms.

Therefore, by the time Paul Jones arrived upon the scene of action, there was very little to be done in the way of murdering.

The Curlew's sides grated against those of the Aimée.

The Curlew was the name of Paul Jones's schooner.

As the grappling irons were thrown, the great freebooter himself leapt on to the deck of the Aimée, with his cutlass flashing in his hand.

Captain Kydd saw him at once.

Quitting the Vampire, he strode across the dead bodies strewn in his path and made his way towards him.

Paul Jones recognised him immediately.

Sheathing his sword, he outstretched his hand towards the pirate captain.

Kydd grasped it heartily.

"What, captain, is it you? Hang me if I could not have sworn it was. I've been chasing this infernal brig since daybreak, and after all the prize has fallen to you."

"No, no!" replied Kydd, hastily. "Dog must not rob dog, you know. The brig sailed straight up to us for protection, and so I seized her for you."

"Oh, that be hanged!" cried Paul Jones, who did not like to be outdone in generosity. "You wholly misrepresent the matter. We, I take it, were two hawks upon the wing, with a single pigeon between us."

"Ha—ha—ha!" laughed Kydd. However, as we happen to be friendly hawks, I must at least press you to share my prize with me. What say you to an equal division of the spoil?"

I accept your offer right willingly," replied Jones." "Upon my word, Kydd, you are quite a princely fellow in your way, and it does my heart good to see you again. It's deuced strange, though, that we should have met to-day, for it was only last night that I was dreaming of you."

"You will think it stranger still when I tell you that for the last four-and-twenty hours I have been wondering when I should be most likely to come across you."

"What! You want to see me particularly?"

"Very particularly, indeed."

"How odd! And here I am ready to serve you, my boy, in any way that lies in my power."

All this while the two captains retained their grasp of one another's hands, and looked each other full in the face.

There was a very marked difference in the pearance of the two men.

So far as personal appearance went, Captain Kydd was far superior to his brother rover.

Paul Jones was rather below the average height.

His features were singularly striking.

His forehead broad—his jaws square and massive—his lips thin—his nose aquiline—and his eyes deep set, small, dark, and piercing.

A quantity of jet black hair descended from beneath his cocked hat.

His costume was that of a captain in the American navy.

But his person was not at all calculated to set off the smart uniform to any great advantage.

His frame was a very powerful one, however, and it scarcely required two glances at his broad, square shoulders, deep chest, and sturdy legs, which were slightly inclined to be bowed, to tell that he possessed an unusual amount of muscular power.

While the two captains were thus exchanging a few words, Nero, with hideous face, and great hands smeared with blood, came panting up.

"Captain."

"Well, Nero?"

"They cry quarter!"

"How many are there?"

"Ten, with the mate," replied Nero. "They are all strapping fellows."

"Good," replied Kydd. "We have plenty for fresh hands to do. On board the Vampire with them."

"Clap them in irons, captain?"

"Most assuredly."

The French sailors were instantly seized and dragged away by the pirates.

Without loss of time they were clapped in irons and consigned to the hold of the Vampire.

Then the work of getting the cargo up from the hold commenced.

A rough division of the spoil was made by Captain Kydd and Paul Jones.

Then the respective crews conveyed the bales and chests to the two schooners.

All being practised hands, surprisingly short work was made of this.

Captain Kydd and Paul Jones looked on until the whole of the cargo was transferred.

"What is to be done with the brig?" asked Nero.

"Scuttle her," replied Kydd.

"Aye—aye, sir!"

Nero, and several ferocious-looking pirates, descended to the hold, where they set to work at once in a most workman-like manner and bored a number of large holes in the bottom of the vessel.

In came the water in most amazing quantities.

"That will do—come on lads," cried Nero.

And he made his way to the deck, which he found quite deserted.

CHAPTER XL.

PAUL JONES DECLARES HIS READINESS TO ASSIST CAPTAIN KYDD, AND THE TWO PIRATES MAKE A VERY BOLD RESOLVE.

CAPTAIN KYDD and Paul Jones lingered not on the deck of the Vampire to see the last of the brig Aimée."

There was nothing novel to either of them in the sight of a good ship slowly sinking with her murdered crew.

They knew that the ocean would swallow up the Aimée, and that in a very short space of time all traces of the awful crime they had committed would have vanished for ever beneath the blue waves which heaved for many and many a mile around.

Nothing more would ever be heard of the brig Aimée.

The owners of the vessel, the proprietors of the cargo, the relatives and friends of the crew—all these people would fail to glean any tidings of the fate of the brig Aimée.

It was quite evident that she would not float for another half-hour.

"So far, so good," remarked Kydd. "Now, Paul, let us pledge one another in brimming goblets.

"With all my heart."

The two famous pirates sat down at the table facing one another.

Then they proceeded to business.

As our readers must have discovered by this time, Captain Kydd was not at all the sort of man to beat about the bush.

He was peculiarly blunt and straightforward in his manner.

Therefore, in his own terse way, he explained to Paul Jones how he was circumstanced.

He neither concealed the extent of the dangers which he wished Paul Jones to share with him, nor exaggerated them in the least.

Indeed, so singularly clear was his description of how matters stood, that when he had finished speaking Paul Jones knew perfectly well the exact position of affairs.

"Whew!" whistled the freebooter. "You are rather awkwardly fixed."

"You think so," said Kydd, with a smile. "Well, I must confess you are right. I am in a fix, and I must get out of it somehow."

"Well, then, I am none the less willing to assist you; and now is the time to prove the truth of my assertion. I am at your service, Kydd, whenever you like, so long as my guns carry shot, or I have a sword to wield. And there's my hand upon it!"

Paul Jones stretched his open palm to Captain Kydd, who grasped it with the greatest cordiality.

"Paul, I shall never forget this; and if ever it is in my power, I——"

"Oh! stuff! Heave ahead."

Thus admonished, Kydd proceeded to explain to Paul Jones how he thought they might, by their united exertions, relieve the island and secure the treasure.

The renowned freebooter approved of the plan at once.

It had two very great virtues in his eyes.

It was simple and bold.

Together they were to return to the island, and give the frigate battle.

A more daring act was surely never dreamt of.

The Revenge, with her treble rows of teeth and fearless crew of British sailors, was a foe which four or five such schooners as the Vampire and Curlew might well have been excused for shunning.

But both Captain Kydd and Paul Jones were really remarkable men.

Two more skilful sailors or courageous commanders could not have been found in any quarter of the globe.

And both relied upon the same thing for success.

That was their ability to handle their crafts during the projected action.

Great had been the experience of both in engagements with frigates.

And they knew by cleverly manoeuvring the guns of the Revenge could be rendered so ineffective as to be almost useless, particularly if the sea happened to be at all rough, as they had every reason to hope it would be.

"I suppose, then," said Paul Jones, coolly, as he filled his pipe, "you mean to commence business at once.

"Most assuredly," asserted Captain Kydd.

And taking a pinch of snuff, he blew his nose with the utmost complacency.

"Do you mind touching that gong, Paul?"

"Certainly not."

Paul Jones struck the elegant little gong on the cabin-table.

A pirate instantly thrust his head in at the door, which he only partly opened.

"Send Nero to me."

"Right, captain."

The head disappeared and the door closed.

Almost immediately, however, it was again opened, and Nero, whose garments were splashed with blood, appeared on the threshold.

"Issue orders for both vessels to get in readiness for a rousing fight, and then make for the island."

Nero stared.

"But the Revenge."

Kydd laughed.

"Do as I bid you, Nero."

"All right," replied the black, who now fully understood why the instructions to get the vessels in fighting trim had been issued.

His great eyes were opened to their fullest extent, and the aspect of his dark visage was grave in the extreme as he closed the door after him.

* * * * * *

Night again closed over the South Atlantic.

And such a night it seemed destined to prove, too, as would be most favourable to the success of our hero's enterprise.

The sky was mantled with clouds, the moon's disc entirely obscured.

There was little fear, indeed, that the fair queen of night would show her lovely face.

There were only a few stars, too, sprinkled here and there, at vast distances apart.

With the utmost care the frigate was steered according to our hero's instructions.

A sharp look-out was kept up on board the Revenge, and Captain Canon, standing upon the quarter-deck, kept his night-glass continually directed towards the island.

No sign of life, however, could be discovered.

The pirates seemed to have abandoned themselves to repose, with a sense of perfect security.

Such, however, was not the case.

All along the beach the pirates kept a keen look-out.

At length the Revenge dropped her anchor.

So far was she from the island that in the darkness it was impossible for the pirates to make her out.

The gig and the cutter were then lowered.

The very best men were selected from the frigate's crew to man the boats.

Our hero was entrusted with the command of the gig.

Hans Van Ryder had charge of the cutter.

Then, with muffled oars, the boats proceeded towards the tall and rugged rocks behind which the brigantine was concealed.

The utmost caution was exercised.

Fortunately the swell was strong.

Therefore, as each man held his tongue, the pirates on board the brigantine heard no sound

As they rounded the rocks the outline of the brigantine could be plainly distinguished by the man-o'-war's men.

But no light could be discovered.

Fore and aft, aloft and alow, all was utter darkness.

In fact, to all appearances, the brigantine was wholly deserted.

Our hero, however, knew better.

Lionel-of-the-Sea was well aware that six pirates formed the smallest complement ever left in charge of the vessel.

number would, in all probability, be doubled.

But the rascals, who generally spent their time in gambling in the principal cabin because it was the most commodious and luxurious, were sufficiently cunning to curtain the windows.

The two boats glided alongside the brigantine.

And now voices and laughter could be heard distinctly.

Little dreaming of danger, the pirates were carousing in the chief cabin, and evidently enjoying themselves to their hearts' content.

Lionel-of-the-Sea unsheathed his cutlass and placed it between his teeth.

Then he drew his pistols, felt the primings with his fingers, and replaced them in his belt.

The example was followed by the crews of both boats.

"Now, my lads," whispered Lionel, "follow me noiselessly, and in less than five minutes the brigantine will be ours."

As he spoke, the gallant little fellow scaled the vessel's side with the agility of a monkey.

Silently as spectres, the blue-jackets swarmed after him.

Lionel waited until all the men were at his heels.

"Ready?" he whispered.

"Ready—aye, ready!" was the response.

"Then come on."

Waving his cutlass over his head, Lionel sent the cabin door flying open and sprang in.

He was followed instantly by Hans Van Ryder and the blue-jackets.

The consternation caused by this sudden and alarming intrusion can be more vividly imagined than described.

The savage miscreants gathered round the table, sprang to their feet.

Exclamations of amazement, yells of rage, and frightful oaths issued from their throats.

Then there was a flashing of naked brands and a clicking of pistols.

"Seize them, lads!" cried Lionel-of-the-Sea; "and those that resist, slay on the spot—Hurrah, we have them now!"

The pirates, however, did not seem at all ready to give in without resistance.

Full well did they know that capture meant death.

And not one of them felt inclined to swing from the yardarm of an English man-of-war.

Therefore, a most fierce and sanguinary fight ensued.

But it was of brief duration.

The British sailors were too much for the pirates.

In less than two minutes the whole of the latter were placed *hors de combat*.

Then the capstan was manned, the anchor raised, and the sails unfurled.

By this time those on the island had evidently discovered the fact that the brigantine had been captured by the crew of the Revenge.

Lights gleamed along the shore.

Boom—boom—boom!

In rapid succession guns were fired.

Owing principally to the darkness, however, the balls went wide of their mark.

The brigantine remained untouched.

"Hurrah!" cried Lionel-of-the-Sea, as they rounded the rocks. "We've beaten the rascals this time, and no mistake. Hip—hip—hurrah!"

On board the Revenge the greatest anxiety was naturally felt.

In a fever of excitement, officers and crew awaited the issue of the night's adventure.

Captain Canon himself was particularly anxious.

From the time the boats started to the moment when they returned, towed by the brigantine, he did not leave the deck for an instant.

It is easy to imagine how delighted he was at the success of his enterprise.

As the brigantine came alongside the frigate the first faint streak of dawn appeared in the east.

A flush of crimson glowed on the distant waves.

"Well done," cried Captain Canon, as our hero once more stepped on to the deck of the Revenge. "The thing could not possibly have been managed better. Your hand, Lionel."

"'Tis there."

And our hero grasped the outstretched palm of the captain.

"We have but one thing more to do before the pirate returns, Lionel."

"To take the island by storm."

"Just so."

"When do you intend to commence the attack?"

"In two hours from now."

* * * * * *

Under an easy pressure of canvas the Vampire and the Curlew progressed through the water at a sufficiently rapid rate to satisfy both their commanders.

They were in the cabin of the Vampire together when Nero entered.

"Ah! What is it?"

"We've sighted a ship which is so far out of the usual course of vessels that she seems to be coming direct from our island."

"By Jove!" exclaimed the pirate captain. "That is rather extraordinary. What sort of craft does she appear?"

"Oh, a little brigantine thing," answered Nero. "And, to tell you the truth, I am inclined to think some of our comrades have managed to give the frigate the slip."

"Nothing is more likely," remarked Kydd, "and if so it will indeed be a most fortunate circumstance, and one we may regard as an augury of good. Come, Paul, come."

The two pirate captains made their way to the quarter-deck at once.

Here Nero and several other ruffians awaited them.

Captain Kydd scanned the horizon in the direction in which he expected to find the brigantine.

She was there sure enough.

But so far off that she could only be indistinctly made out with the naked eye.

The celebrated pirate at once brought his powerful glass to bear upon her.

Attentively he regarded the brigantine for several minutes.

Meanwhile not one word was spoken.

On the quarter-deck of the Vampire a positively breathless silence prevailed until Kydd broke it.

"It is her, sure enough."

"The Petrel, captain?" inquired Nero.

"Beyond all doubt."

The Petrel was the name by which the brigantine had been christened by Captain Kydd himself.

"Then it may be taken for granted, I suppose," said Paul Jones, "that she is manned by your men, who have managed to baffle the vigilance of the cruiser."

"Certainly."

Not the slightest doubt was now entertained by anyone on board the Vampire as to the distant brigantine really being the Petrel.

Captain Kydd most certainly could not be mistaken.

And none suspected for an instant that the Petrel was manned by others than pirates from the island.

If anyone had ventured to suggest that she was manned by English men-o'-war's men, and commanded by Lionel-of-the-Sea, he would most assuredly have been regarded as a raving maniac.

Yet such was really the case.

The direction of the two schooners was slightly altered, in order that they might in the ordinary course of things come right athwart the Petrel's bows.

The distance between the two schooners and the brigantine rapidly decreased.

Then the movements of the latter began to occasion some surprise on board the two former.

Over the bulwarks leant our hero, looking out to sea, but the distance was too far for him to be recognised by his enemies.

Indeed, the crew of the Vampire were extremely puzzled.

Instead of recognising the Vampire, as the pirates naturally expected they would, their supposed comrades began to show unequivocal signs of alarm.

Some of the Petrel's sails were taken in

The yards were squared, and then away she began to cut before the wind, in a direction which would quickly carry her far out of the line at present taken by the two schooners.

To account for this strange conduct on the part of the Petrel the pirates were wholly at a loss.

Surely the crew of the brigantine could not have mistaken the Vampire for any other vessel, or entertained the smallest doubt as to her identity.

"Confound them, for a set of fools!" cried Captain Kydd, testily. "What the devil do they mean?"

"Can't make out," replied Paul Jones; "their movements are most peculiar."

"Cursed strange, you mean," cried Kydd, who was getting decidedly wrath. "Now, then, there, crowd on all sail. Hard-a-port. So, that will do nicely. Damme, we shall be close enough to them presently, I'll wager."

The utmost energy was now displayed by the pirates on both schooners.

Soon the two vessels were flying along before the wind at a most astonishing rate.

Hitherto the Vampire and the Curlew had kept close to one another.

Now, however, the superior sailing qualities of the former were displayed in a most striking manner.

The Curlew was quickly left behind.

Sail after sail was crowded on, until her tall and taper masts bent like whalebone beneath the tremendous pressure.

And the gallant little craft sped onward like an arrow.

The chase now became really exciting.

The curiosity of the pirates was fully aroused.

All sorts of speculations were rife on board the Vampire.

"Curse catch them!" cried Kydd. "What the devil can be their motive? Curse me if I don't think they've gone stark staring mad!"

"Who do you suppose is in command of her?" inquired Paul Jones, who had been watching the movements of the brigantine with keen interest for the past few minutes.

"Can't say—I am fairly puzzled."

"Whoever it is?" remarked the American, "he is a thorough sailor, and handles his craft in such a manner as convinces me he will make it a hard matter for us to get hold of her in spite of the Vampire's speed."

The more this fact forced itself upon the pirate captain's mind the more puzzled he became.

At length, however, a faint suspicion of the truth dawned upon him.

The brigantine was not manned by his men at all.

But if not, by whom?

His heart almost stood still as he asked himself the question.

If manned by men from the Revenge, the most alarming inferences were to be drawn from the fact.

After all, perhaps Paul Jones's assistance had been procured too late.

Captain Kydd still maintained his stand on the quarter-deck of the Vampire.

CHAPTER XLII.

LIONEL-OF-THE SEA AND CAPTAIN KYDD ONCE MORE COME FACE TO FACE.

CAPTAIN KYDD gazed searchingly above and around.

Overhead there now hovered not a cloud.

Neither speck nor stain marred the cerulean beauty of the heavens.

The gale had subsided to a brisk breeze, which caused the schooner to leap through the waves like a thing of life.

In spite of the persistent efforts of the British Government to put a stop to Kydd's lawless and audacious proceedings the celebrated pirate had met with no little success.

In fact, at the time at which we are writing Captain Kydd was in the very zenith of his fame.

"Sail ho!" sang out the man in the fore-top.

In an instant the pirates were thrown into a state of excitement.

Hither and thither they ran; priming pistols, loosening cutlasses in there scabbards, and piling boarding-pikes, ready to be clutched at an instant's notice.

"Where away?" demanded Captain Kydd.

"Off the starboard bow!"

Captain Kydd clapped his glass to his eye.

Nero, the black and gorgeously attired lieutenant, hastened to his side.

A number of pirates swarmed up the rigging, leaped on carronades and other convenient places, and eagerly scanned the ocean as far as their practised eyes could reach.

Then there appeared, far away in the distance, a speck of white, so small that it might easily have been mistaken for a sea-gull.

But well did the pirates know it was a ship.

But what kind of vessel would she prove to be?

A merchantman or a frigate?

That was the anxious question which rose uppermost in the minds of all.

A moment of suspenseful silence ensued.

"Well, captain," inquired Nero. "What do you make her out to be? Is she the Revenge?"

And Nero glanced somewhat anxiously into Kydd's face.

Captain Kydd did not reply immediately.

Every pulse beat high with excitement.

Then Captain Kydd took the glass from his eye and closed it with a snap.

"She's a Dutchman."

This somewhat contradictory assertion was received by the pirates with a lusty cheer.

"Now lads, look sharp, clap on every rag of canvas and let us see how swiftly the Vampire can swoop down upon her prey."

Another cheer from the men.

Then the snow-white sails of the saucy schooner bellied out before the breeze until the long and raking masts bent like reeds beneath their pressure.

Under a perfect cloud of spotless canvas the Vampire scudded along at a most amazing rate.

The Vampire had been built expressly for speed.

And she proved to be the swiftest sailing vessel afloat.

Hence it was that the pirate had been able to set the law at defiance for so long.

No threat could deter him—no chasing could catch,
For the Vampire had never yet met with his match.

All was now activity on board.

The guns were loaded and run out, and every preparation make for the coming fight.

And now in the bustle, eagerness, and excitement, no one gave a single thought to the vessel which, up to this moment, they had been following.

With heart elate stood Captain Kydd upon the quarter-deck of the Vampire, which seemed actually to fly along, as she clove through the foaming water, and dashed the spray from her beautiful prow.

He whistled a light and lively air as he drew his flashing blade, and bent it almost double, as if proud of its exquisite temper.

Then he fixed his gaze impatiently upon his intended victim.

By this time the distance between the two vessels was so greatly decreased that the Dutchman could now be plainly discerned.

It was a brig.

Little did her captain suspect the nature of the schooner.

He made no attempt whatever to alter the direction of his brig until the two vessels were actually quite close to one another.

Then the long grim-looking tier of guns on the starboard side of the Vampire caught his attention for the first time.

The Dutchman in a moment showed very evident signs of alarm.

There was a sudden commotion on her deck.

Captain Kydd applied his glass to his eye again.

He could now distinctly see all that was going on on board the brig.

The crew were running about in wildest excitement and terror.

The captain stood upon the poop, waving his arms frantically as he shouted forth his orders.

Then the brig's yards were squared.

She veered round.

More canvas was cracked on, and she began to sheer off at a very good pace indeed.

A low, mocking laugh came from the pirate's lips.

"As well might a dove hope to escape the swoop of a falcon," said Kydd to Nero, as the Vampire veered round also. "Up with our flag, and let them see who it is that follows in their wake."

Even as the command was given the black waving folds of the pirate's dread ensign fluttered to the mast-head.

Then, as it streamed out upon the breeze, a white figure standing in its centre became visible.

This was a very gracefully-formed snow-white kid on a black ground.

Well was that terrible flag known and acknowledged as the scourge of the seas.

And in vain did the Dutchman try to outstrip her fleet pursuer.

Every instant perceptibly diminished the distance between the two vessels.

"What do you say to trying a shot at her?" suggested Nero, as he rested his hand upon one of the bow-chasers.

"We'll give her a hail first," replied Kydd. "A-h-oy!"

Captain Kydd's lungs might have been made of leather, so strong were they.

Such a hail as he gave them must have been heard by everyone on board the fugitive craft.

But no notice was taken of it.

"A-a-hoy!" cried Captain Kydd. "Heave to, or, curse me, I'll sink you. I am Captain Kydd, the pirate!"

This announcement, however, had no other effect upon the captain of the Dutchman than to induce him to risk the spreading of a little more canvas, although there had already been more unfurled than the brig could carry with safety.

Several of the pirates now rushed forward to work the bow-chasers.

Captain Kydd himself directed the weapon:

"Now blaze away!"

The order was at once obeyed.

A flash of flame.

A cloud of smoke.

Boom!

Eagerly the pirates awaited the result.

A loud crash announced that the shot had told.

When, indeed, did a ball from a gun directed by Captain Kydd fail to reach its mark?

The Dutchman staggered and shivered from stem to stern like a wounded deer.

The utmost confusion prevailed upon her deck.

"Fire again, lads! Just cripple her, so that after we have overtaken the Petrel we can come back and secure our prize."

The miscreants cheered lustily.

And so well did they do their work that in a very few minutes the Dutchman was rendered mastless, and lay like a log upon the water.

Of course her captain and crew fully expected that the pirate would come up alongside at once.

Therefore their surprise was great indeed when they saw the yards of the Vampire suddenly squared round, and the ship sail away, leaving them afloat upon the ocean a perfect wreck.

"Now Paul, my boy—we'll join in the chase again. The Curlew has a fair start of the Vampire now, but I shall be very much astonished if she keeps the lead until the cursed brigantine is overhauled."

Paul Jones laughed.

"Between us, it will be odd if we do not manage to capture such a cockle-shell as the Petrel."

The chase of the Petrel now momentarily grew more exciting.

Captain Kydd watched the flying brigantine with feverish anxiety.

Each moment his alarming suspicions as to the crew with which the Petrel was manned grew stronger.

But even yet he was far from guessing the whole truth.

Still the time was not far distant when he was destined to make a most startling discovery.

Rapidly both the schooners gained upon the little bark.

Captain Kydd and Paul Jones kept their glasses constantly on the fugitive, which they would have overtaken long ago, but for the magnificent seamanship displayed by her dauntless young commander.

Suddenly Captain Kydd started with surprise and almost dropped his glass.

An exclamation left his lips.

A cry, half of amazement, and half of joy.

"Aha! cried Paul Jones; "you have made a discovery?"

"An astonishing one."

"So it seems."

"Surely," said Captain Kydd, "I am neither mistaken nor labouring under a delusion—and yet it seems too good to be true. Let me look again."

And once more he clapped his glass to his eye.

"What is too good to be true?" inquired Paul Jones.

"By Jupiter! it is true," replied Captain Kydd, now evidently labouring under extreme excitement. "Hurrah! hurrah! hurrah!"

Paul Jones stared at him in wonder.

"What on earth is the matter?" he demanded. "Have you suddenly gone mad?"

"Not quite," said Captain Kydd; "but now I understand how it is the brigantine has given us so much trouble."

"The deuce you do."

"Yes. Do you see standing on the poop a slender and graceful figure?"

"A youth very tastefully attired?"

"The same! Well," replied Captain Kydd, "that is the commander, though how, in the name of old Davy, to account for his presence in that capacity, or in any other, I am wholly at a loss."

"Who is he, then?—looks young to be a captain."

"Nevertheless, there is not a smarter sailor afloat."

"He is my pupil—that ungrateful young cub of whom I spoke to you yesterday."

"Lionel-of-the-Sea?"

"Lionel-of-the-Sea," averred Captain Kydd. "And by my soul he shall not escape my vengeance this time."

And he gave fresh orders to the crew.

Both the Vampire and the Curlew were now gaining hand over hand on the brigantine.

For the latter to escape was simply impossible.

The issue of the race was now but a question of from fifteen to twenty minutes.

At the expiration of that time either of the schooners would be able to reach her with a shot.

Nero advanced, and, hearing the news, communicated it at once to the crew.

It was received with shouts of delight.

There was no consummation more devoutly

desired by the bloodthirsty miscreants than our hero's destruction.

The knowledge that he was on board the Petrel increased ten thousand times their anxiety to overhaul that craft.

But how he came to be in possession of it was a circumstance of which they were wholly unable to find any satisfactory explanation.

All sorts of alarming speculations arose in their minds.

One and all were filled with alarm concerning the island.

And they trembled to think what their fate would be if they blindly sailed into the bay, and found themselves caught like rats in a trap.

Soon, however, would they know the worst.

Suddenly from the Curlew's bows there came a puff of white smoke, followed by a crash and a roar.

It was only a trial shot at the fugitive.

And, although it did no damage, the projectile proved that the Curlew, at any rate, had the Petrel within the range of her guns.

It plunged into the water only a few yards from the Petrel's stern.

But the brigantine was armed also, and, hopeless as the encounter was, at once showed fight.

The fire was instantly returned, and with such accuracy of aim that the projectile carried away a portion of the Curlew's bows.

Paul Jones uttered a curse.

Captain Kydd laughed.

"Lionel fired that shot, for a wager," he cried. "And you will see he'll fight against all odds, as long as he has a plank to stand upon."

"He's got some grit in him, then?"

"You may well say so. Oh, Paul, you don't know how bitterly disappointed I am in that boy. He was always so full of promise, and loving him as I did for his ready wit and daring spirit, I used to look forward with pride to the day when he should fight side by side with me, and become as renowned as myself."

"But you could not make a pirate of him?"

"No Paul," replied Captain Kydd, in accents of real regret. "And yet I have tried by every possible means."

"And all in vain?"

"Yes, all in vain! And worse than vain, for all he knows he owes to my careful training; and how has he used his knowledge? By endeavouring, with its aid, to encompass my destruction."

"Humph! A clearer case of black ingratitude never came under my notice," said Paul. "But this time you will not let him slip through your fingers?"

"No—by my soul!—his hour is at hand. This day the viper dies. Ah! now we will try a shot."

Captain Kydd at once issued the necessary order, and an iron ball went flying over the space between the Vampire and the Petrel.

This shot took effect—carrying away the brigantine's jibboom, and doing other damage as well.

At the same moment, too, a second projectile

from the Curlew went crashing into the starboard side of the ill-fated little craft.

Thus the Petrel was completely crippled.

Captain Kydd waited until he was within hailing distance, and then shouted through his trumpet—

"Petrel ahoy!"

"Vampire ahoy!" was the answering hail.

"Strike your colours! It's all up with you this time, Lionel-of-the-Sea."

"Never!—miscreant!" retorted our hero.

And now the utmost activity was displayed on board of the saucy Petrel.

In an amazingly short space of time the canvas was sheeted home and the deck cleared for action.

Evidently her devoted crew were bent on fighting to the last gasp, and meant to die in their attempt to repel boarders.

The three ships were now very close together.

Never was there a prospect of so desperate and hopeless a fight.

Lionel-of-the-Sea had only a crew of twenty-five hands, all told.

But these twenty-five were stalwart and steady tars; men who knew not fear and never gave a thought to odds.

That they would indeed make a gallant fight both Captain Kydd and Paul Jones knew full well.

The fact that they were really some of the Revenge's crew did not fail to create exceedingly lively sensations in the breasts of Captain Kydd and his followers.

It did indeed look as if the island had already been taken by Captain Canon and his blue-jackets.

"It so," muttered Kydd, "it is all the work of that accursed young devil's imp. But, at any rate, revenge is at hand, and he shall die like a dog, though I die the next hour. Ah, here we are."

The sides of the three vessels grated together.

"Hurrah!" cried Kydd, as the grapnels were thrown. "Follow me—no quarter—mind, no quarter!"

"Aha, Lionel, we meet once more—and for the last time."

And flourishing his sword, the pirate captain leaped to the Petrel's deck, on to which at the same moment there came pouring swarms of ferocious rascals, who, with horrible cries and threats, rushed upon the gallant band of heroes, who met them in grim silence.

Then arose the horrid sounds of strife.

Right well and nobly did each gallant tar defend himself.

Lionel-of-the-Sea met the murderous onslaught of the savage boarders with unquailing courage.

He was suddenly attacked by a black pirate with a long iron spear; but with that wonderful coolness which never deserted him in the most trying moments he avoided the crushing blow by stepping nimbly aside, and shot the ruffian through the throat.

For each blue-jacket who fell the bodies of half a dozen pirates were stretched upon the deck.

But even then the unequal battle could not long be maintained.

One by one the dauntless defenders of the

Petrel were stricken down.

Captain Kydd and Lionel-of-the-Sea, singling each other out, fought once more foot to foot and hand to hand.

Paul Jones stood calmly by, and watched with evident delight this splendid exhibition of swordsmanship.

In spite of the accounts which Captain Kydd had given him of our hero's prowess, Paul Jones fully expected that when the duel commenced in real earnest his grim old comrade would quickly bring it to a conclusion.

But the manner in which Lionel foiled Captain Kydd's most deadly thrusts and cunning feints filled him not only with surprise but admiration.

Fainter and fainter became the sounds of resistance on the part of the Petrel's crew.

Louder and louder the yells of rage and triumph in which the pirates indulged.

With fiendish joy the cowardly hounds beheld the valiant fall.

And still the passage of arms between the pirate chieftain and our hero continued.

The only advantage gained by either of the combatants was claimed by our hero.

He had inflicted an ugly gash on the side of Captains Kydd's right temple.

From this the blood flowed freely.

Paul Jones emitted a long, low whistle.

As he did so, to his unbounded astonishment, he saw Captain Kydd's weapon wrenched from his grasp, and sent whirling right over the bulwarks.

With an audible sound it fell on to the Vampire's deck.

At the same moment a wild cry of terror and despair burst from the lips of the pirate crew.

This was not to be wondered at, for a great and sudden change had taken place in the conflict.

The deck of the vessel was now swarming with spectre-like forms, and as Lionel-of-the-Sea saw the gaunt form of Vanderdecken appear and rush headlong at Captain Kydd, the brave lad uttered a great shout of welcome.

Overcome with astonishment the pirate chief recoiled. He slipped, and fell prone upon the deck, and before he could recover himself Vanderdecken's foot was upon his chest.

"Ha, ha!" the spectre laughed, "you are in my power at last."

"You lie!" Captain Kydd hissed. "You have no other power than to haunt and torture me."

"See!" cried Vanderdecken, raising his arms aloft.

Captain Kydd followed the motion with his eyes, and to his dismay he saw the black flag, bearing the skull and cross-bones, running down, its staff broken in twain, and the sombre bunting hanging in limp folds.

Down came the much-dreaded flag until it fell with a dull thud upon the deck, and Captain Kydd uttered horrible curses as he saw Lionel-of-the-Sea trample upon it.

"His hour of triumph is but a brief one," the fierce pirate yelled. "He shall die a hundred lingering deaths for this."

"Base wretch!" the spectre cried, "you only prolong your agony."

"Then," said Captain Kydd, "my time has not yet come. You confess it. I defy you, foul mockery."

While this was going on Paul Jones found himself hard pressed.

Stricken with a mortal terror at the appearance of the spectre crew, he fled.

For once his courage deserted him, and he sought safety below.

Suddenly he heard a shout.

It came from Captain Kydd.

"The ghost has vanished," he cried, "and left me to deal with Lionel-of-the-Sea! Now, lads, you shall see how I will deal with the whelp."

Ashamed of his weakness, Paul Jones hurried on deck, and saw that Lionel-of-the-Sea and Captain Kydd were once more engaged in a passage of arms.

The appearance of Vanderdecken convinced Lionel that no great harm would come to him, and he fought like a young lion.

Yet he was puzzled for a reason why the spectre should have left and withdrawn his ghostly crew at such a critical moment.

Perhaps the action was to make the lad faithful and self-reliant.

Lionel advanced step by step, beating showers of sparks from Captain Kydd's sword, until the pirate was fairly tired.

Then our hero delivered a tremendous blow at the villain's head.

"Ha, ha!" laughed Lionel. "Take that."

Captain Kydd fully expected that moment to be his last.

But some evil genius seemed for ever to watch over the marauder's life.

Clash!

And the death-stroke was arrested by another weapon.

"All right, Kydd!" sang out Paul Jones. "This lad fights well."

And he at once commenced a vigorous attack upon our hero, who, although taken so entirely by surprise, had yet managed to recover his guard in time.

"There is an acknowledgment of the compliment, miscreant!"

And he drew blood from the Yankee's shoulder.

Paul Jones gave a shout of fury.

"Bring this devil's imp down, Kydd. Why waste more time? Ah, that was well done, Sancho."

This remark was brought forth by the action of a long, lean, slinking rascal, who aimed a fearful blow with a marling-spike at our hero from behind.

Lionel dropped his sword—staggered and fell.

"Bring that cub on board the Vampire," cried Kydd. "And then fire the barque before quitting it."

"But why not leave him to the flames?" inquired Paul, with some surprise.

"Because I should never feel sure that he had really perished," replied Captain Kydd. "And I mean to leave no room for doubt as to his fate this time. Bear a hand, there, and bring the boy along."

The last of the defenders had fallen some minutes.

"I've fired the ship!" cried Nero, appearing on deck at this moment.

His assertion was quite sufficient.

In less than a minute the deck of the brigantine was cleared.

Lionel's senseless body was flung rudely on to the deck of the Vampire.

Then the grapnels were removed, and the two schooners parted company with the doomed brigantine.

So our hero's scheme was thwarted.

So perished Captain Canon's most sanguine hopes.

If he waited for the Juno until the Petrel brought her his patience must be great indeed.

CHAPTER XLIII.

LIONEL-OF-THE-SEA WALKS THE PLANK.

NEITHER the Vampire nor the Curlew lost any time in giving the doomed brigantine as wide a berth as possible.

"How did you fire the ship, Nero?" inquired Paul Jones.

"Oh!" replied the sable warrior, with that nonchalance he so usually affected when he was not in a rage, "there was a keg of powder in the hold, so I took nearly a whole candle from a lantern and lit it."

"And you stuck the tallow end in the powder, I suppose?"

"I buried it a good inch deep," answered Nero, with so much gravity and simplicity, that even the great American pirate was staggered.

"Whew!" he whistled. "What if a spark had fallen."

"It is my practice to fire ships in that manner whenever I can, and Captain Kydd approves of it. Two score and more have I served the same way, and no spark has fallen yet."

"Do we go in search of the Dutchman now?" inquired Paul of his compatriot.

"Assuredly!"

Captain Kydd issued the necessary instructions, and orders were given to the officer commanding the Curlew to keep that vessel beside the Vampire.

"Meantime," said Nero, all arrangements being made, "what do you propose to do with this offspring of Satan?"

And with his great foot he spurned our hero's apparently lifeless body.

Lionel groaned.

"He lives," hissed Nero.

And his eyes gleamed savagely as he drew his kreese.

"Hold!" cried Captain Kydd.

"What, captain! Would'st spare him again and allow him by some mysterious juggle to escape —as he has escaped before," growled Nero. "Believe me there's no time like the present. Here he lies! Here's my blade! 'Tis but one stroke and the deed is done effectually! The head once fairly severed from the trunk and never can the breath of life roll through the nostrils."

"True, Nero—true," agreed Kydd; "but I want first to obtain some information of him. How do we know at present whether the island is still in the hands of the garrison we left? Things wear an ugly look, and I would fain be satisfied upon that point—so banish that scowl and put up your blade."

Surlily enough Nero obeyed.

Captain Kydd stooped over the handsome boy and saw that already a pool of blood had collected beneath his head.

The pirate knelt down and gently raised Lionel to a sitting posture, supporting him with his right leg.

"Is he not a picture, Paul?" inquired Kydd. "A tawny lion's cub! Ah! It's a thousand pities his notions should be so misguided! However, regrets are useless, and this day Lionel must die —Ralph."

"Aye—aye, sir."

A gaily bedecked youth, of attractive appearance, at once hastened up, and made a not ungraceful bow.

"Water in a basin and some linen for a bandage."

"Aye—aye, sir."

Ralph lost no time in fetching the required articles.

Then Captain Kydd himself bathed our hero's head and washed his hair, while Nero looked on with a smile of mingled amusement and contempt.

Having bandaged the boy's head with as much skill as a well-practised surgeon, the pirate tore open our hero's doublet in order to place his hand immediately over the heart.

As he did so, a large piece of white paper, carefully folded, fell on to the deck.

"Ah!" exclaimed Kydd. "What have we here?"

And still supporting our hero, who now began to exhibit some faint signs of returning consciousness, Kydd picked up the document.

He hastily unfolded it.

Paul Jones watched him narrowly.

What did that sudden change of expression on the pirate captain's countenance mean?

As he hurriedly perused the document smiles beamed from every line and wrinkle of his face.

"What is it?" inquired Paul Jones, eagerly.

"Something well worth dragging this young rascal on to the Vampire's deck for," replied Kydd; "for it sets at rest all the doubts and fears which have so recently arisen."

"You don't say so! What is it?"

"A despatch from Captain Canon of the Revenge to Captain Marchmont of the Juno. Egad, 'twas lucky, indeed, we managed to fall foul of the Petrel. Read it for yourself."

And he handed the document to his friend.

"Stars and stripes!" commented Paul Jones. "Dame Fortune seems to have made a special favourite of you, Kydd."

"She does, indeed."

"If we had sailed to the bay and found two English frigates instead of one ready to lock yards with us, what then?"

"We should have met with a very disagreeable surprise. And you see who planned it."

"Lionel," said Paul Jones. "And how highly Captain Canon praises him. The captain of the brigantine is fully described here. What a daring young dog he is!"

"A sea-lion, rather."

"Well, sea-lion then. I perceive that you admire that boy in the same manner that you do the king of beasts."

"Just so. And shall kill him for the same reason that I should slay a lion."

"In order to preserve your own life?"

"Exactly. Ah!"

Lionel inhaled a deep breath and opened his eyes.

Dreamily he gazed about him.

Then a low moan broke from his bloodless lips.

"Brandy," said Kydd, "brandy. A good dose will put new life into him for a time, and I wish him to be conscious at the moment of his death, in order that it may be embittered by the knowledge of my triumph."

"Here you are."

Paul Jones handed Kydd the large silver flask which he invariably carried in one of his capacious side-pockets.

The English pirate at once applied the neck of the bottle to our hero's mouth.

Slowly the potent spirit trickled down his throat.

It produced an almost immediate effect.

After a fit of coughing a faint tinge stole back into his cheeks.

His eyes brightened considerably.

And ultimately he actually reared himself right up, and sat without support.

"Where am I?" he murmured at length, "and what has happened?"

He passed one hand across his brow, and then gazed round as if dazed and bewildered for a moment.

Then his eyes encountered those of his arch enemy.

He recognised them at once, and they seemed to produce quite an electrical effect upon him, for with a bound he sprang upon his feet.

Drawing himself erect, with his head thrown proudly back, and his long silk-soft tresses floating wildly about his shoulders, he fearlessly confronted his foe.

"So, monster! I am once more upon the deck of your accursed craft."

"Yes, boy, and in my power! Captain Canon will be finely disappointed when he finds that the Petrel has failed in her errand, and the Juno does not join him in the bay."

"Possibly; but that will not prevent him from ultimately accomplishing his purpose. Even though I do not live to see it he will nevertheless surely convey you to London in irons; for I have heard from one who long ago has shaken off the mortal coil what your end will be. It is written in the book of doom."

"Liar!"

"You can call me what you like, pirate; but to alter the decree of fate you will find beyond your power."

"Pish!"

"You will hang at Tyburn, Captain Kydd."

"Ha, ha, ha!"

"Laugh as long and as loudly as you like—such will be the ignoble end of Captain Kydd!"

"Never!" cried Kydd livid with passion. "Say rather that I shall go down to some coral tomb in the ocean's bed—amidst flame and smoke—fierce and free to the last!"

"I should be a false prophet if I did."

"You lie."

And Captain Kydd's face flamed with fury.

"I repeat it—and you will remember my words when the time comes—yes, Captain Kydd, you will hang by the neck until you are dead, and in your last moments hear not, as you fondly imagine, the clashing of swords and the thundering of guns, but the yells and groans of execration of a mighty multitude."

"Then," shouted Kydd, hoarsely and with a volley of frightful oaths, "you at least shall not be there to scoff and gibe! Ahoy there, hearties! Bear a hand here and bind this young viper! Rig a plank and run it out at once."

A number of pirates had already gathered round to witness the interview, and instantly Lionel was seized from behind.

Weak and faint as he was from the loss of blood, he could offer no effectual resistance.

Quietly, therefore, he submitted.

The miscreants bound him securely enough.

Their confederates as deftly rigged the plank and ran it out in wonderfully quick time.

They were practised hands at this sort of work.

"Ready?" inquired Kydd.

"Aye! aye! captain."

"Then make him march. Farewell, Lionel. Go and feed the fishes! To fill the hungry is an act of grace."

And Kydd waved his hand.

Then the pirates seized Lionel, and with unnecessary violence urged him to the plank.

Our hero was propelled past the centre.

CHAPTER XLIV.

CAPTAIN CANON AND THE ENTIRE CREW OF THE REVENGE ARE SURPRISED IN A TRULY STARTLING MANNER.

THE plank on which Lionel was balanced in mid-air tipped up.

"Hurrah!" cried Captain Kydd. "He has gone at last! So, after all, ends the career of Lionel-of-the-Sea."

Our hero vanished in the ocean with a sullen splash.

That Captain Kydd vainly hoped he had put an end to the adventurous career of Lionel-of-the-Sea by forcing him to walk the plank it is scarcely necessary to inform our readers.

Had not Vanderdecken given our hero a charm which rendered the ocean powerless to injure him?

And the potent talisman which had saved him

so many times from a watery grave failed him not now.

As he plunged into the waves Lionel became at once unconscious.

How long he remained so of course he was never able to determine, but on returning to his senses he found himself lying in his own berth on board the Revenge.

Sitting up, he gazed wonderingly about him.

Every object which encountered his eyes was perfectly familiar.

Then he examined his own person.

The ropes with which the pirates had bound him so unmercifully had been removed, and the wounds he had received in that terrible and unequal engagement with the Vampire and the Curlew all carefully dressed.

He felt dazed and bewildered, and placed his hand to his throbbing and aching brow.

It was strapped up with a surgical bandage.

Then, after a little reflection, he inhaled a deep breath of relief.

"Once more," he said, "once more do I owe my life to that mysterious being who has ever proved so faithful a guardian to me. And now what shall I do? Seek Captain Canon, and give him an account of that unfortunate mischance by which I fell in with Captain Kydd and Paul Jones?"

And he left his bunk.

On doing so he staggered and nearly fell.

It was only by clutching the side of the bunk he saved himself.

Lionel was indeed very weak.

The amount of blood he had lost was alarming.

He felt that to reach the deck would cost him a most desperate effort.

Still, he must endeavour.

Fortunately there was in his locker, amongst other things, a bottle of brandy, and to this he helped himself.

At any other time he would not have ventured to drink so deeply as he did then of the raw spirit.

But the brandy he knew would inspire him with strength and energy, which, however artificial, would yet enable him to accomplish his purpose.

"Ah!" he muttered, as he replaced the bottle and closed the locker, "I feel already like a different being. I can surely walk now."

He stood up, and moved towards the door.

Although still somewhat unsteady on his legs, a glow of satisfaction warmed his heart as he found himself able to get on so well.

Yet it was with slow and painful steps he made his way upwards to the deck.

Several times he paused, and wondered what effect his unexpected appearance on board the Revenge would produce.

At length he reached the top of the companion ladder.

For the last time he halted and listened.

Evidently the strictest order reigned on deck.

Scarcely a sound reached our hero's ears.

"Ha!" thought Lionel, as a faint smile wreathed his bloodless lips. "The captain is on deck if I am not very much mistaken. Never-

theless, his presence will not restrain the commotion I am about to cause."

And boldly he stepped on to the deck.

As he did so a variety of sounds broke the silence, which, a moment before, had been most complete.

Exclamations of astonishment.

Cries of horror.

The tramp of feet and a hundred other noises greeted our hero as he emerged from the hatchway.

All this, however, was nothing more than Lionel-of-the-Sea had expected.

"Fear not!" he cried, stretching forth his arms, and shaking the long wet curls which escaped from the bandage about his shoulders. "I am Lionel-of-the-Sea, and I am in the flesh!"

This statement, however, was regarded by the crew with no small amount of incredulity.

The sailors, who knew no fear of death, come how death might, never failed to experience the greatest and most unaccountable terror at anything which savoured of the supernatural.

And surely everything connected with the appearance of Lionel-of-the-Sea at that moment was such as favoured the impression that he was no mortal being.

His wild, weird aspect.

The deathly pallor of his face heightened by the ensanguined bandage on his brow and the intense brilliancy of his eyes.

His drenched hair and clothing, from which the water dripped so freely that already there was a pool at his feet.

All this, and the fact that he was supposed to be miles away on board the Petrel, tended, indeed, to give colour to the notion of his being a visitant from the land of spirits.

Consequently the wildest terror and confusion prevailed on the deck of the Revenge.

As for Captain Canon and several of the officers who happened to be on the quarter-deck, they were thunder-stricken.

They stared aghast at the singular figure which had so unexpectedly emerged from the hatchway.

For several moments neither ventured to express any opinion.

Hans Van Ryder was the first to speak.

"Surely," said he, "it is Lionel come back again."

"Yes," coincided Captain Canon. "But how?"

"He must be dead," suggested the first lieutenant. "Depend upon it, some disaster has overtaken the Petrel. She has fallen in with the Vampire, and in that case it is not hard to imagine what would ensue."

"Her captain and crew butchered, and the vessel sent to the bottom of the ocean," said another.

"Ah!" exclaimed Hans Van Ryder, "and this is Lionel's spirit come to let us know what has happened."

And now a hush, sudden and profound, came over the deck of the frigate.

Frozen with nameless terror, the sailors stood around in various attitudes—motionless and speechless.

The situation was a strange one for Lionel-of-the-Sea.

Weak and giddy from the loss of blood, it was only natural that he, too, should feel confused and be undecided how to act.

Therefore, he stood all this time in the very position he had taken up on leaving the top rung of the companion-ladder.

A more novel or startling scene than the deck of the Revenge presented at that moment cannot easily be imagined.

And now ere another word was spoken, and before any one had moved hand or foot, the door of the state-cabin was thrown open and a fairy-like form came forth.

Our hero recognised in an instant those angelic features and that figure of ineffable symmetry, and the semblance of a flush overspread his visage as he cried aloud—

"Violet—dear Violet!"

Violet Eversleigh uttered a scream, and, to the amazement of the crew, rushed towards him.

"Lionel—Lionel!"

Another instant, and Violet Eversleigh was clasped in our hero's arms.

And then, for a moment, that fond and faithful pair seemed to forget utterly and entirely all things around them.

"Violet," murmured our hero.

"Dear Lionel! Is it you? Oh, what has happened? You are wounded? And how came you here—speak—speak. Something terrible has taken place. Tell me all—tell me all."

Lionel endeavoured to make some reply, but could not.

The greatness of his emotion was too much for him.

His power of speech was gone.

All he could do was to kiss her again and again, while murmuring—

"I—I—can't tell you yet—by and by, love—by and by."

As she spoke Vanderdecken appeared, and Lionel started back.

"Farewell," the spectre said, approaching Violet and taking her hand. "It is well that you do not tell Lionel all yet, for though I bid you farewell, my mission may not be at an end."

Before Violet could reply the spectre had vanished, and Lionel amazed stepped forward.

"Did you mark him?" Lionel said. "I never saw his face wear so pleased an expression."

"Dearest," Violet replied, "we are surrounded by mysteries. Let us talk of ourselves."

It would seem, however, that the appearance of Violet Eversleigh upon the scene at that moment was most opportune.

The meeting of the lovers served, in a great measure, to dissipate those awful suspicions entertained by the officers and the superstitious fears of the crew.

In all probability there was not one man on deck who did not experience some sensation of shame at the weakness he had displayed on witnessing the unhesitating way in which a fragile little girl had approached the seeming apparition from which they one and all had shrunk in dread.

"We must see what all this means," said Captain Canon.

"That it is Lionel, alive and wounded, there can be no doubt," said Hans Van Ryder; "but how he got in such a plight, and by what means he reached this ship, is a mystery."

"A mystery indeed," echoed the first lieutenant.

"But one that Lionel will be able to explain," said Captain Canon, "so let us greet him."

And he at once descended the steps leading from the quarter to the main-deck.

Hans Van Ryder and the officers accompanied him.

The sailors, whose fears had in a measure subsided, though they still felt anything but at their ease, watched them approach the main hatchway, near which our hero and heroine stood, with breathless suspense.

Lionel had observed the approach of Captain Canon and the officers.

Therefore he gently disengaged himself from Violet's embrace, and saluted them with due respect.

"You are surprised to see me," he said, with a faint smile, "are you not?"

"Surprised, Lionel! We are amazed—bewildered—fairly lost in a fog," declared Captain Canon. "And really you must admit that your unexpected appearance requires a little explanation."

"It seems to have caused a considerable sensation," replied our hero; "but, believe me, I had no intention whatever of causing you such a shock, I—I—have much to tell you, but am wounded and weak. I——"

Lionel reeled and nearly fell.

Hans Van Ryder caught him in his arms.

Violet Eversleigh uttered a scream.

"He is dead—dead!"

She would have thrown herself upon his breast, and bathed his pale face with her fastly-flowing tears, had not Captain Canon gently restrained her.

"No, Violet; calm yourself. He is wounded, and severely, I fear, but he will recover."

"You think so?"

"I feel sure he will. Some special providence must watch over this boy's life, dear, or he never could have passed through what he has." Then, addressing Hans, he asked, "How does he seem, Mr. Ryder."

"His heart," replied the young Dutchman, "beats but feebly—he had better be handed over to the doctor."

"Very good."

"Here is the doctor," said the first lieutenant, as a tall, handsome, well-proportioned man, joined the group.

"Another patient for you, Dr. Simpson," said Captain Canon. "Get him round as quickly as you can, for he has some important information in regard to Captain Kydd."

"Great Powers!" exclaimed Doctor Simpson, as he bent over our hero, who was now lying on the deck with his head resting on Hans Van Ryder's knee. "It is your young protégé—

Lionel-of-the-Sea."

"Exactly."

"And how, in the name of wonder, came he here?"

"That is a matter as yet unexplained. However, let no time be lost. Come and report his condition to me as soon as you are able."

"I will."

Lionel was, at Doctor Simpson's order, carried below.

He still remained insensible.

Violet Eversleigh was with difficulty prevailed upon to retire to her cabin, and then Captain Canon turned to address the crew.

"My lads," he cried, "there's nothing to be alarmed at, so make your minds quite easy, and so soon as the doctor has got the boy round you shall know all about it."

"Captain," said one of the men, stepping forward and touching his forelock, "is it Lionel-of-the-Sea?"

"It is."

"And not his ghost?"

"He is no more a ghost than you are. I give you my word for that."

The sailor saluted and retired, after which a more general feeling of satisfaction evinced itself.

The men of the Revenge knew their skipper, and placed implicit reliance in his assurance.

Still their mystification and curiosity was not abated in the least.

In fact the excitement of the crew was such that scarcely any one of the men knew what he was doing.

To and fro they moved restlessly—pale and perplexed, like the phantoms of a ghastly dream.

When they spoke it was in whispers.

Meanwhile, Captain Canon retired to his cabin, flung himself into a chair, planted his elbows on the table, and buried his face in his hands.

He, too, was troubled.

And perhaps more so than any of his crew, though his ideas—however vague—were much nearer the truth than theirs.

An hour passed by.

Only an hour, and yet to the commander of the Revenge it had seemed like twelve.

Suddenly he looked up.

Rat-tat-tat.

A knock at the door.

"Come in."

The door opened and Doctor Simpson stood upon the threshold.

"Well, doctor, what of your patient?"

"He has so far recovered," was the reply, "that he will be here directly; however, be careful to check any excitement on his part, for he is in a fearfully weak state, being literally covered with wounds."

Captain Canon nodded assent.

"I wish to be alone with him," he said. "But do not go far away, if you fear a sudden relapse."

Footsteps were now heard without.

"He comes," said the doctor. "If I am wanted the sentry can call me. I shall be within hail."

"Good."

The captain waved his hand, and the doctor retired.

Scarcely had he done so when another knock resounded on the panel.

CHAPTER XLV.

THE TUG OF WAR.

CAPTAIN CANON having given permission, the cabin-door was gently opened, and several blue-jackets entered, carrying Lionel-of-the-Sea in a hammock.

"Place him on the couch," said the captain.

This was done.

The sailors were then dismissed, and once more Captain Canon and our hero were alone in the state-cabin of the Revenge.

The former regarded Lionel with a searching glance.

Very pale and weak the handsome and gallant youth looked, as, propped up with cushions of crimson velvet, he reclined on the couch in a listless yet graceful attitude.

He would have raised himself upon his elbow, but Captain Canon bade him remain quite still.

"The less you exert yourself, my lad, the better," he said, kindly.

Lionel smiled.

"I am not quite so badly hurt as you seem to think, captain, and in a few hours hope to feel very different to what I do now. A little rest and nourishment will make a wonderful difference in me."

"Doubtless, and now——"

"I know what you would ask," interrupted Lionel. "And, with your permission, will give you a full and complete account of all that has happened to me and the ill-fated crew of the Petrel."

"Ah! The Petrel came to grief."

"Her crew died like heroes," replied Lionel. "The last man was cut down fighting."

"And the Petrel?"

"She was blown up."

"By whom?"

"The pirates—Captain Kydd and Paul Jones."

Captain Canon elevated his eyebrows, and looked at our hero as if he could scarcely credit the fact of the great American pirate being in conjunction with the still more celebrated Captain Kydd.

"Yes, Captain Canon, Paul Jones. He and Kydd are hand and glove—in a word they have entered into an alliance offensive and defensive, and entertain sanguine hopes of being able to grapple with you in a most successful manner."

"Ha—ha—ha!"

Captain Canon was forced to laugh.

"Well, Lionel, go on with your story—tell it from the beginning to end, and then we shall be better able to understand the exact position of affairs."

Lionel did as he was requested.

In simple language, and without the least exaggeration, he detailed all that had transpired since the ill-fated Petrel parted company with the frigate.

But the exertion of speaking was almost too great for him.

In fact, he would not have proved equal to the task had not Captain Canon, who watched him closely, supplied him from time to time with a small quantity of wine.

Leaving Lionel to rest for awhile upon the couch, Captain Canon leaned back in his chair and thoughtfully twirled his moustache.

"But how?" he inquired, at length, "did you manage to regain the Revenge after the blowing-up of the Petrel?"

"You must keep my secret if I reveal it to you."

"On my word of honour."

"That is sufficient. Vanderdecken gave me a talisman long ago, and more than once before it has saved my life in such emergencies. See, here it is."

And plunging his hand into his doublet, our hero displayed the treasured and priceless charm.

Then for some time did the gallant captain and the fearless boy talk matters over.

Contrary to the expectations formed by the doctor, and shared by Captain Canon, Lionel, so far from being distressed by the interview, seemed to be rapidly recovering.

The result of this confabulation was, that the commander of the Revenge determined to alter his tactics.

He requested Lionel to give him the fullest possible particulars concerning the position and probable movements of the pirates.

"For dy'e see, my lad," said he, smiting his solid thigh, "those rascals on the island cannot get away until their comrades come and fetch them, and if we can only come athwart-hawse with the Vampire and the Curlew, it will be easy enough to make a general attack on the island afterwards."

"True," cried Lionel, "and if no time is lost I think we shall be able to steal a march on Captain Kydd and Paul Jones, for they imagine I am at the bottom of the ocean, and dream not that you have the slightest inkling of their whereabouts."

"True—true," replied Captain Canon. "We will weigh anchor at once. I am going on deck now. Will you be all right where you are?"

"Quite right."

Captain Canon left him to give the requisite orders.

Scarcely five minutes had he been absent when Lionel knew, from the cheery sounds and the regular tramp, tramp, tramp overhead, that the capstan bars were manned and the anchor being weighed.

In fact all seemed tumult overhead.

While he was listening to the shouting of the officers the responses of the men and a hundred other noises only to be heard on board a frigate at such times, the door of the cabin was opened silently and a slender figure glided in.

Our hero raised his eyes, and a smile of pleasure irradiated his face.

It was Violet, who, availing herself of the busy occupation of the crew, had stolen, unobserved, to her lover's side.

Kneeling beside the couch, she twined her arms around his neck, and pressed her fair, soft cheek against his own.

Their eyes met.

And, though Lionel was wounded and Violet wept, both were happy.

We will leave the lovers to themselves—as all lovers like to be left at such times—and join Captain Canon and Hans Van Ryder, and the officers of the Revenge on deck.

It was now about four o'clock in the afternoon.

The weather still continued the same.

The ocean was calm.

The sky cloudless.

Yet there was sufficient breeze to fill the sails of the frigate, and waft her onwards at a rate that left nothing to be desired.

Captain Canon had given the best possible explanation of Lionel's appearance to the crew, who were delighted to learn that the pirate of whom they had been in search for so long a period was so near at hand.

"Well, captain," said Hans, "you think there is a prospect of success at last?"

"Oh! yes; if I am not mistaken we shall manage to come up with the villains this time. You see that infernal rascal Kydd will not be so anxious to avoid an encounter now that he has a consort of so formidable a character as Paul Jones."

CHAPTER XLVI.

PROSPECTS OF A FIGHT.

"CERTAINLY not. Still he would hardly seek an engagement if it could be avoided."

"I am not so sure of that—Lionel seems to think that these two pirates have come to the conclusion that together they are a match for us."

"So much the better if true."

"And they are both men of great daring."

"Very great daring," agreed Hans Van Ryder. "But when they have to match themselves against such an enemy as the Revenge they only fight as rats fight when they are driven into a corner."

"True—but if the breeze should stiffen and the night prove dark, who shall say that when the grey light of dawn steals over the ocean we shall not find ourselves actually within range of the miscreants?"

"Such a thing is possible."

"Quite possible, Hans. And—ha! the breeze, as if in answer to my wish, grows livelier every moment."

This was indeed the case.

The wind was rising.

Before the freshening breeze the Revenge, with stud-sails set, ploughed through the waves with majestic speed.

Hour after hour flew by.

And still Captain Canon kept his stand on deck.

In fact he had determined not to leave it until

the sun had set and the shades of evening caused the horizon to contract to such an extent that he could not possibly see a distant sail.

In the interim, Lionel-of-the-Sea had been carefully attended to, not only by Violet Eversleigh, but also by Dr. Simpson, who seemed very much pleased and surprised at the rapid progress his patient was making.

The doctor wished to remove him to his own berth, but Lionel expressed a desire to remain where he was, which, being communicated to Captain Canon, was assented to.

Violet, however, seemed to think that her lover was anything but in a fair way to recovery, and at length she summoned up courage enough to follow the doctor out of the cabin.

"Tell me the truth," she said, laying her hand on his arm, and looking up into his eyes, "Is he really in danger?"

"Not in great danger, though what has happened to him would undoubtedly have killed most men."

"And you do not think he will die?" asked Violet, eagerly.

"I do not! He seems to be made of iron, or something tougher, so do not alarm yourself, Miss Eversleigh! Under my care he will soon grow quite sound again."

"Oh, thank you, thank you, for that assurance."

With a much lighter heart Violet stole back to her lover.

Lionel was sleeping peacefully, and so she sat down by his side to watch and wait until he awoke.

Shortly afterwards Captain Canon entered.

"Ah! you still with the patient, Violet?"

"Yes! And I want you to grant me a favour."

"Well, what is it?"

"Let me be his nurse to-night."

"Will it not fatigue you too much?"

"Oh, no! I am sure I shall not feel tired in the least. Indeed, if you dismiss me I shall have no rest."

"Ah, well, I suppose you must have your way, wilful little tease that you are. I shall make a few entries in my book, and then retire."

Captain Canon committed to paper the incidents of the day, and then sought his couch for the night.

Thus Violet and Lionel were left entirely alone. Our hero slumbered.

CHAPTER XLVII.

YARD-ARM TO YARD-ARM WITH THE PIRATES.

"SAIL ho!" sang out the man at the masthead of his Britannic Majesty's frigate, the Revenge.

"Where away?" demanded Captain Canon.

"Off the starboard bow."

Captain Canon clapped his glass to his eye, the officers clustered round him, and great excitement was immediately manifested by the crew.

This was increased when the man on the lookout announced that another sail had made its appearance.

Doubts, if any were entertained, resolved themselves into certainties.

"That's the Vampire, sure enough," said Captain Canon.

And closing his glass with a snap he shouted his orders to the crew.

Every stitch of canvas was stretched to the breeze, and the Revenge ploughed the waves in grand style.

Rapidly the distance between the frigate and the two schooners was decreased.

The latter appeared to entertain no dread of the frigate's approach.

So far from displaying any smyptoms of fear, or exhibiting any desire to seek safety in flight, they coolly furled their sails, and Captain Canon, who had once more resorted to his glass, exclaimed—

"Why, shiver my timbers, if the lubbers are not clearing the decks for action! They mean to give us battle!"

"Then will they pay dearly for their temerity," remarked the first lieutenant.

"But will fight like fiends from hell," said Hans Van Ryder. "It will not do to underrate their offensive powers—they mean mischief."

That Hans Van Ryder spoke the truth no one doubted.

The prospect, however, of having a final engagement with the pirates of whom they had been so long in chase filled the crew of the Revenge with enthusiastic delight.

In feverish excitement they waited until the schooners were within hail.

The pirates had made no attempt at disguise.

The black flag with the kid's head and crossed antlers floated from the saucy Vampire's masthead.

And the stars and stripes streamed from the Curlew.

"Surrender!" bawled Captain Canon through his speaking-trumpet. "Haul down that infamous rag, or we will blow you from the surface of the sea."

"Never!" retorted Captain Kydd. "Blaze away like hell, if you choose. We defy you!"

And as the fierce pirate spoke a puff of smoke burst from the bows of the Vampire.

Boom!

Crash!

The well-directed shot struck the Revenge, and carried away a portion of the lee bulwarks.

The splinters flew around, and several of the jolly tars received from them slight injuries.

Beyond this, however, no damage was done, and another ball, coming this time from the Curlew, flew harmlessly through the rigging, and fell with a sounding splash into the ocean.

Captain Canon hesitated no longer.

"Now, lads, let them have it. Give each a round."

The Revenge at once replied to the challenge of the pirates, and soon a perfect storm of grape hissed through the air, and the three vessels were enveloped in a misty shade of death.

The pirates' guns were worked splendidly.

Great was the havoc occasioned in the gun-room of the frigate.

CHAPTER XLVIII.

VICTORY !

BUT in her turn the Revenge made the two schooners suffer.

In spite of the manœuvring of the Vampire and Curlew the Revenge got nearer and nearer to them as the time wore on.

Soon it became evident that the pirate vessels had not the ghost of a chance of escaping.

The superior sailing qualities of the Revenge rendered it certain that she would come up with the pirate in the course of another half-hour.

The decks of the vessels were cleared for action and all the guns loaded to their muzzles.

Captain Kydd, however, in spite of his assured success, seemed strangely moody and silent.

He scarcely spoke one word until the Revenge was actually within range of the Vampire's bow-chaser.

He himself superintended the working of this gun.

It was brought to bear upon the Revenge's mizenmast.

Kydd took his sight with care.

Then he held up his left hand.

"Fire !"

Boom !

There was a flash of flame and a cloud of smoke.

Boom !

Anxiously the pirates looked for the result.

It did not quite realise their expectations.

Kydd's aim had been at fault.

"Revenge !" Kydd shouted in a rage. "Ahoy ! Heave to or we'll sink you !"

As the stormy voice of the celebrated pirate died away there came a jet of white smoke from the stern of the vessel, and the next instant a heavy shot plashed into the water, so close beneath the schooner's bows that it is a wonder no mischief was done.

That was the only reply Lionel-of-the-Sea sent to Captain Kydd's demand.

"Death and destruction !" roared the pirate. "What the devil do they mean ? Surely they will not be so mad as to give us battle."

"One would hardly think so," replied Paul Jones, who had come aboard. "But, nevertheless, I must confess it looks marvellously like it. Ah, here comes another !"

And as the American buccaneer ceased speaking there was another jet of smoke from the Revenge—this time from one of the larboard guns, as already the position of the vessels was materially altered.

This second shot proved more effectual than the first.

It carried away a portion of Vampire's lee bulwarks, and although the shot itself did no further damage, two of the pirates were severely hurt by the splinters that went flying in all directions.

Captain Kydd swore a frightful oath.

"By Jupiter, the fellows have some pluck !" he cried. "Bah ; as sure as my name is Kydd they shall pay dearly for that shot. Now then, lads, let them have a broadside."

"Aye, aye, sir."

And the Vampire's guns poured forth their thunder and smoke.

That the broadside was a well-directed one was at once evident, for the Revenge was seen to heel half over.

"Egad, that was enough to sink her," cried Paul Jones.

"Strike !" yelled Captain Kydd, as the Vampire now rapidly neared the Revenge. "Strike ! or I will blow you out of the water in another minute."

To this the Revenge replied by running up the Union Jack, and returning the broadside with such good effect that considerable damage was done to the Vampire.

"Let them have it, lads !" cried Kydd.

A second broadside was delivered by the Vampire ; but little harm was done.

Fore and aft were the Vampire and the Curlew raked by the death-vomiting guns of the mettlesome frigate.

In fact, all three vessels were so crippled that hostilities ceased for a time.

Captain Kydd was in anything but an amiable frame of mind.

Closing his cabin door he paced to and fro with folded arms and wild, uneven steps.

His eyes rolled fearfully, and as he ground his teeth together, as if he meant to reduce them to powder, a white foam gathered round his lips.

Dark were the thoughts which rolled through his mind at that time, and his proud heart swelled as if about to burst when he thought of the peril he was in.

Oh ! that was gall and venom, indeed.

He could scarcely contain himself.

Paul Jones had gone on board the Curlew to see that things were going on in their proper order.

Therefore, the celebrated pirate had no one to view him in that moment of supreme convulsion until the inner door opened, and Zulu half emerged from the adjoining cabin.

Then she stood in the doorway, and stared at Captain Kydd in amazement.

Never had she seen him so disturbed before.

"What ! angry ? Not love Zulu ?"

And her beautiful brows contracted in a frown.

Kydd paused abruptly in the centre of the cabin, and regarded her half sternly for a moment.

Then his features softened a little, as a something which bore a semblance to a smile appeared upon his visage.

He shook his head, and turning upon his heels began to pace about again when Zulu's voice once more interrupted him.

This time she spoke, her dusky little fingers were on his shoulder, and her coral lips quite close to his ear.

"Tell me—what ?"

And as he turned round she fixed her large expressive eyes upon him.

Zulu's knowledge of English was still very limited, though with but little tuition she had made wonderful progress.

Therefore when she spoke it was in such quaint sentences that rarely anyone but Captain Kydd could have understood her.

And as we cannot possibly convey by words the faintest idea of the changeful expression of her voice and features, it is better that we should convey her meaning in such words as all may readily understand.

"That accursed boy," hissed the pirate, trembling with concentrated fury. "Would he were dead."

"Catch him again and kill him," suggested Zulu, in a soothing and gentle voice.

Kydd shook his head.

"Would that I could."

"Could? What!"

Zulu drew back and looked at him with her eyes open to their fullest extent.

Then there came a look over her lovely and ever-changing features which expressed as plainly as words.

"Oh, I understand; there is some reason why you must not kill him."

The next words she spoke convinced Kydd that such was the idea which had flashed into her mind.

"Could? Ah, well—see I will—I can. I will meet him on deck when the fight comes, and kill him there."

And holding up one finger impressively she drew her scimitar and moved towards the cabin door with soft and stealthy steps like those of a pantheress about to pounce upon her prey.

"Hold!" cried Captain Kydd, "Zulu, Zulu, you know not what you would do. You must not go."

At this moment Nero appeared, and announced that the Revenge was preparing to attack.

This was indeed the case, and Captain Kydd reached the deck in time to see the vessels close, and the grapnels thrown.

Then ensued the most terrific hand-to-hand fighting Captain Canon had ever witnessed.

Hans Van Ryder's prediction was fully verified.

The pirates did indeed fight like fiends.

No quarter was asked.

In fact to implore it would be vain.

Death was the doom of all who fell.

And amidst the terrible tumult three forms became remarkably conspicious.

The forms of Captain Kydd, Paul Jones, and the gigantic black lieutenant of the Vampire.

The latter presented a most hideous spectacle, as he strode over the dead and dying, his hands and feet all red, and with brains spattered over his face.

Thus he came face to face with Captain Canon, who gripped a cutlass in one hand while he grasped a pistol in the other.

Full in the negro's face he presented the latter.

There was a flash and bang.

Nero uttered a yell, and falling backwards on the blood-stained deck, died with a curse upon his lips.

Meanwhile Captain Kydd was, according to his custom at such times, exceedingly busy.

Up to the hilt was his cutlass dyed with blood.

and as Nero fell he rushed upon the commander of the Revenge.

With a loud clash their blades met.

"Demon," said Captain Canon, "we meet at length. Yield; you are my prisoner!"

"Never," retorted Kydd, "no topsman* will ever turn me off."

"Thou liest!" sounded a loud clear voice in his ear.

Kydd started as if he had been stung.

Surely he knew those accents.

Lionel-of-the-Sea with his head bandaged, and a sword in his hand, strode up.

Captain Canon disarmed the pirate, and sent his sword whirling over the bulwarks. Kydd staggered and fell to the deck.

He had swooned.

"Clap him in irons," shouted Captain Canon. "This is the pirate, Kydd. Now then, lads, look sharp. We have him at last!"

"Hurrah!"

A ringing cheer greeted this announcement.

The pirate captain was carried to the deck of the Revenge at once.

The news that he had been taken spread like wildfire, not only amongst the blue-jackets, but the pirates also.

And the effect it produced was wonderful.

The pirates seemed suddenly to lose all heart.

With astounding ease the man-o'-war's men struck them to the deck.

"I have done with this," cried Paul Jones.

And he blew shrilly upon a whistle.

This was a preconcerted signal.

At once all those who belonged to the Curlew made the best of their way back to their own ship.

Availing themselves of the excitement of the moment, the Yankees, cloaked by the clouds of sulphurous smoke that overhung the vessels, threw off the grapnels as silently as possible.

Then like a spectre the Curlew glided away.

Some time elapsed ere this circumstance became generally known, owing to the last stand made by the pirates of the Vampire.

Soon, however, all was over.

Captain Kydd and half-a-dozen of his blood-thirsty crew—all suffering more or less from wounds received in the fray—were loaded with chains and safely lodged in the hold of the Revenge.

"And now," remarked Captain Canon to the officers who had gathered around him, "we have only to dispose of this schooner."

"We cannot leave her as she is," said the first lieutenant—"her blood-drenched decks all strewn with corpses."

"Certainly not."

"One moment," Lionel said. "There must be something on board this vessel relating to myself. Who will follow me to Captain Kydd's cabin?"

"I will," the doctor of the Revenge said.

They went down together, the doctor lighting a candle, for it was growing dark, and the vessel was full of smoke.

"Here," cried Lionel, breathlessly, "here is the trunk I have seen Captain Kydd looking into so often."

Our hero overturned the contents of the trunk, and thrust several bundles of documents into his breast.

"I am ready now," he said. "This accursed vessel shall no longer float the seas."

"There is plenty of powder on board, I'll be bound," said Lionel to the captain, as he returned on deck, "and there could be no more appropriate termination of the Vampire's cruise than a general blow-up."

"You mean, fire the magazine."

"Certainly. Let the pirate-ship go down wrapped in flame and smoke."

"With all my heart," said Captain Canon.

"Then my hand shall do the deed," cried Lionel.

And away he sped to the powder-chamber.

Meanwhile preparations were made for the ships to part company.

"'Tis done," cried Lionel-of-the-Sea.

And he bounded on to the deck of the Revenge.

"Hurrah!"

A tremendous cheer resounded through the frigate as the grapnels were thrown.

Great activity was displayed by the crew, who were exceedingly anxious to get as far away from the doomed ship as possible.

"The Revenge," remarked Lionel-of-the-Sea, "is not the first vessel that has sought to give the Vampire a wide berth."

"By no means," assented Captain Canon.

"In less than another minute she will blow up," said Lionel, "The piece of lighted tow I left in her magazine must be nearly burnt through."

"Perhaps," suggested Hans Van Ryder, "it has gone out?"

"Yonder flash settles the question!" cried Lionel.

And he pointed towards the crippled schooner.

Even as he spoke the sound of a tremendous explosion rent the air, and fire and smoke issued from the Vampire's sides.

Far and wide were hurled the fragments of the pirates' matchless schooner.

And when the flare died out and the smoke cleared away all that remained of the Vampire was a few charred embers which in black masses floated here and there.

"Captain Kydd's career as a pirate has come to an end," said Lionel-of-the-Sea.

"But," observed Captain Canon, "as a criminal it has yet to terminate."

"Which it will eventually do at the end of a rope, or I am not a true prophet," avowed Lionel. "And now I suppose we return to the island!"

"Sail ho!" sang out the man at the masthead.

"Where away?"

"To starboard!"

Captain Canon swept the horizon with his glass.

A cry of astonishment broke from him—

"The Juno, by thunder!"

CHAPTER XLIX.

THE ATTACK ON THE PIRATES' ISLE.

THIS announcement was received with shouts of surprise and lusty cheers by the crew of the Revenge.

The Juno was sailing in their direction, and so came rapidly in sight.

"She must have heard the explosion, if not the firing," said the first lieutenant.

And this proved to be the case.

Ere long the Juno and the Revenge were close alongside.

"So you have settled the rascal at last," said Captain Harvey, as he shook hands with the commander of the Revenge, on the quarter-deck of that vessel.

"Thank heaven, yes," replied Captain Canon. "But there is something else to be done."

"And what may that be? If I am rightly informed Kydd is a prisoner on board this vessel, and the Vampire has blown up—in fact, it was the sound of the explosion which induced me to sail in this direction."

"That's right enough, Harvey. But that rascal, Kydd, owns a strongly fortified island, where his treasures are deposited."

"Well?"

"And on that island the remainder of the crew are still regaling themselves. Shall we leave the rascals there, and with all that wealth?"

"No—decidedly not!" responded Captain Harvey. "We'll deal with the miscreants—elevate them to the yard-arm, if that's all."

"And stow the treasure in our holds."

"By all means."

Captain Canon and Captain Harvey then entered into a long conversation.

But although the discussion was one of an exceedingly interesting and edifying character we have not space to publish it here.

For the purposes of our story it will be sufficient to say that the two captains arrived at a mutual understanding.

They agreed, without loss of time, to attack the pirates' isle.

Thither the two frigates sailed in company.

Meanwhile strict watch was kept upon Captain Kydd.

By one he was watched continually.

And that one was Hans Van Ryder.

"You slew my father," said the young Dutchman; "and I will see you hanged."

And Hans Van Ryder kept his word.

However, we must not anticipate.

The Revenge and the Juno made a most successful assault upon the pirates' isle.

Stoutly were they resisted by the buccaneers.

But all to no purpose.

Eventually the pirates had to give in, and such of them as survived the conflict were consigned to the holds of the two frigates, in which they were destined to make a voyage to England in chains.

Then commenced a search for the vast treasure which Captain Kydd was known to have hidden somewhere.

We ne d scarcely inform our readers that that search was entirely unsuccessful.

Weeks were wasted in fruitless endeavour.

All sorts of expedients were resorted to, to induce the pirates to disclose the secret place in which their hoard was hidden.

One and all remained firm.

Vain alike were threats, promises, and punishment.

Nothing could induce them to divulge the secret.

Indeed, Captain Kydd had previously taken the precaution to extract an oath from each, of such a nature that even they—pirates and murderers as they were—dared not break.

Therefore, the skipper's arguments and the bo'sun's rope's end proved alike unavailing.

The Revenge, having accomplished her purpose, sailed straight for England.

On the homeward voyage our adventurers were favoured with remarkably fine weather.

During the voyage, Lionel-of-the-Sea—who rapidly recovered from the wounds he had received in his gallant defence of the Petrel—and Violet Eversleigh were more together than they had ever been before.

And never were two lovers happier than they.

While homeward bound there happened only two incidents of a startling nature.

Captain Kydd made a desperate and nearly successful attempt to escape from his confinement, and thwart the hangman by leaping overboard.

And it was owing entirely to the vigilance of Hans Van Ryder that the famous pirate was thwarted.

The young Dutchman's vigilance alone safeguarded the custody of Captain Kydd.

"All right," cried Hans, during the hubbub caused by the pirate's desperate though futile attempt to escape. "All right—he's safe enough."

And safe enough he was.

But what was the other incident ?

It was one of a still more startling character.

And one more worthy of record.

It was a beautiful moonlight night, and the Revenge was rounding the Cape, when Lionel-of-the-Sea awoke from a long and peaceful slumber.

Through the cabin-window the moonlight came in a beautiful broad stream, and making the place light.

By its aid our hero became aware of the presence of one to whom he was already deeply indebted.

A tall, stately, and spectral form stood beside his bunk.

The phantom of a handsome man, arrayed in costume that had been in vogue two centuries and a half before.

In a word it was Vanderdecken.

A faint smile rested on his wan features, and his right hand was thrust in the breast of his doublet.

"Strange and mysterious friend," cried Lionel-of-the-Sea, "you are always a welcome guest to me. May I inquire if any special object is the cause of this visit ?"

"Yes," replied Vanderdecken, in that singularly mournful manner to which our hero had grown so accustomed. "For one thing, I am come to bid you farewell."

"Farewell ?"

"Aye—farewell !" answered the spectre, with a sigh. "Your destination is London and mine Amsterdam. As the Revenge sails into the Thames the Flying Dutchman will go down in the Zuyder Zee, and never more be seen."

"I thought——," Lionel paused.

"What ?" inquired Vanderdecken.

"That—that," stammered our hero, "you were doomed to beat about until the day of Judgment."

"So I was—as a punishment for my own wickedness and folly, but thank heaven at last, after many weary years, I have obtained a remission of my sentence. I am forgiven——however," he added, after a thoughtful pause, "it was not to discuss this matter I sought you."

"What then ?" demanded our hero.

Vanderdecken withdrew his hand from the breast of his doublet, and held up something which Lionel-of-the-Sea recognised at once.

It was the sealed packet which Vanderdecken had shaken so threateningly in the face of Captain Kydd on that memorable night, when, amidst all the tumultuous horrors of the tempest, Lionel had been cast overboard.

Even in that moment of dreadful excitement Lionel felt conscious that the contents of that mysterious packet were in some way connected with his fate.

Nor had his instinct misled him.

"What have you there ?" inquired Lionel, as with eagerness and curiosity he gazed upon the sealed packet which the spectre exposed to his view.

"That," replied Vanderdecken, "which will prove of infinite advantage to you ! Examine well these papers when I am gone. They are the proofs of your birth, parentage, rank, and fortune."

"Parentage ! Rank ! Fortune !" gasped Lionel-of-the-Sea, whose heart pulsated with strange emotions.

Vanderdecken inclined his head in assent.

"And my parents—my mother—my father !—"

The spectre sighed, and pointing downwards, said——

"In each other's arms they sleep the ancient sleep of humankind, and their tomb is a coral cave on the sandy bed of the ocean."

"Ah ! they were drowned ?"

"Yes ; and you were saved by the man who at the great day of judgment will have to answer for their murder—and for many others."

"Ah ! you mean Captain Kydd ?"

"Yes, I allude to that man of blood and infamy," said Vanderdecken. "And now I must bid you a long farewell."

"Shall we never meet again ?"

"Not in this world ! Here are the papers."

And he held them towards our hero.

Lionel's fingers eagerly closed upon them, and as he did so Vanderdecken melted away in the moonlight like a vapour.

"And so," exclaimed Lionel, "I have seen the last of Vanderdecken! Well, he has been a good friend and true to me, and so I rejoice in the knowledge that his sufferings are drawing to a close. Peace to thy bones, O Vanderdecken, when they rest at length in the bed of thy beloved Zuyder Zee. And now to see what I have here."

And nervously he tore open the sealed packet.

It contained a variety of documents.

All were of a most important character.

Lionel-of-the-Sea pondered over them for hours, and even then could scarcely realise the truths thus strangely revealed to him.

"So, so; my real name is Lionel, it seems," he said; "but it has got a handle to it—and such a grand one too—ha, ha! How pleased dear Violet will be when I inform her of the fact, and won't Captain Canon and Hans Van Ryder and all the others stare when they hear my name in full. Lord Lionel Laurelle, ha, ha, ha! What fun! And so the poor ocean waif suddenly discovers that he is a personage of very great importance indeed, a nobleman with a fine estate and a rent-roll of vast proportions. Ha, ha, ha, and so I'm a lord—Lord Lionel Laurelle, ha, ha, ha!—And I've no doubt that rascal Kydd has known it all along."

We need scarcely say that our hero obtained not another wink of sleep that night.

The news spread through the frigate like wildfire, and when our hero made his way on the deck he was hailed by the jolly tars with lusty cheers.

Captain Kydd heard the lusty cheers, and wondered what in the name of goodness was the matter.

"What the dickens is up?" he inquired of Hans Van Ryder, when that vigilant young Dutchman, having congratulated our hero, went to see that his prisoner was safe.

"Something that will make you open your eyes, Captain Kydd."

"Indeed."

"And in truth! Lionel has discovered a packet of papers—the proof of his birth and parentage—and in order to celebrate the event Captain Canon has ordered a double share of grog to be served to all on board."

"The devil!" exclaimed Kydd, with a curse. "But it cannot be," he added, after a thoughtful pause. "The papers went down with the good ship, and must have rotted long ago! No, no—I won't believe it—it is some trick, in order that on reaching England he may set up as an impostor."

"You lie, Captain Kydd. Your foster-child is Lord Lionel Laurelle, as you are perfectly well aware."

"Laurelle!" echoed Kydd. "It must be so then. He has the real papers; though how he obtained them is a mystery to me. His name is Laurelle, and he is Lord Lionel."

"And you have known this all these years, villain!"

"Aye," replied the manacled pirate, "and

meant to have turned it to good account some future day. But 'tis too late now."

"Yes, Captain Kydd, it is indeed too late."

And leaving the pirate captain to his rage, mortification, and chains, Hans Van Ryder went to seek our hero.

He found him on the quarter-deck.

Violet Eversleigh was by his side.

"I suppose," said Hans Van Ryder, "that it is all arranged now?"

"What?" inquired Lionel, while Violet blushed deeply and looked down.

"That question you know to be unnecessary," replied Hans. "My meaning is not to be mistaken. I allude to your marriage with Violet—that is all arranged, is it not?"

"Well, yes. If we reach England in safety, the interesting ceremony will be gone through."

"And the adventurous career of Lionel-of-the-Sea will terminate in a glorious peal of bells."

"And what," inquired Violet, glancing up with a bright smile upon her fair young face, "and what could be better?"

"Nothing," admitted the young Dutchman.

"You shall be my best man," said Lionel. "And now I shall know little rest until the shores of England rise to view. Heaven grant that the breeze continues fair and free as it is at present, until our voyage is ended.

"Amen," whispered Violet.

The voyage from the Cape of Good Hope to England was made in the shortest time on record.

Captain Kydd and eight of his men were safely lodged in Newgate, and Lionel's prophecy was in due course fulfilled.

Not in flame and smoke, bleeding from shot and cutlass wounds—as he had fondly dreamed—did the celebrated pirate terminate his existence.

But before a vast crowd, who had hooted and pelted him all the way from Newgate to Tyburn, did Captain Kydd expiate his crimes upon the gallows-tree.

In justice, however, we must observe that Captain Kydd was game to the last.

A few seconds before being "turned off," he took snuff with the hangman.

And now we have little more to add.

Merely to record the fact that our hero, after going through all the legal formalities necessary, proved his right to the title and estate of Lord Lionel Laurelle.

His marriage with Violet Eversleigh followed as a matter of course, and he was shortly afterwards called to the House of Peers.

Long and happily they lived in our hero's ancestral halls, and the name of their descendants is legion.

THE END.